Margery Hollis

Anthony Fairfax

A Novel: Vol. III.

Margery Hollis

Anthony Fairfax
A Novel: Vol. III.

ISBN/EAN: 9783337002213

Printed in Europe, USA, Canada, Australia, Japan

Cover: Foto ©Andreas Hilbeck / pixelio.de

More available books at **www.hansebooks.com**

ANTHONY FAIRFAX.

A Novel.

IN THREE VOLUMES.
VOL. III.

LONDON:
RICHARD BENTLEY AND SON,
Publishers in Ordinary to Her Majesty the Queen.
1885.

ANTHONY FAIRFAX.

PART II.—*Continued.*

CHAPTER XXII.

'Liebe
' Kennt der allein, der ohne Hoffnung liebt.'
Don Carlos.

RS. CARLYON was quite as angry about Helen's refusal of Fairfax as Helen had expected her to be; and the first days after the terrible news had been broken to her were

ANTHONY FAIRFAX.

PART II.—*Continued.*

CHAPTER XXII.

'Liebe
'Kennt der allein, der ohne Hoffnung liebt.'
Don Carlos.

RS. CARLYON was quite as angry about Helen's refusal of Fairfax as Helen had expected her to be; and the first days after the terrible news had been broken to her were not pleasant ones. Helen heard much of her own senseless folly, and many gloomy pictures—rich in detail—were drawn of the certain future which awaited a girl who displayed such utter incapacity to guide her affairs with discretion.

Mrs. Carlyon was so disgusted that she professed herself unequal to facing the neighbours.

Helen had made herself the talk of the place by her shilly-shallying and weakness, her headstrong determination to have her own way, and her stupid vacillation; and her aunt could not endure to be questioned about the shameful business, and to be condoled with on her niece's— here Mrs. Carlyon paused and shot a glance at Helen as if pondering the advisability of using the adjective she had in her mind, and seeing still the quiet indifference which was Helen's armour in these encounters, went on desperately—her niece's disgraceful and unwomanly conduct.

Even this sharp thrust did not prove a palpable hit. Helen did not appear in the slightest degree ashamed of herself, and only repeated gently: 'Indeed, aunt, I am sorry to displease you; but I couldn't help deciding as I did.'

To escape the condolences and comment which she dreaded, Mrs. Carlyon resolved upon immediate retreat, and went to London, where she took rooms. Her husband must pass his time ashore there; he should not be worried by visiting the scene of Helen's misdeeds, and hearing from his acquaintances of all she had thrown away. He would feel it far more than Mrs. Carlyon did, as Helen was his own relation and he cared so much for her welfare—not that Mrs. Carlyon had not always been as kind to Helen as if she were her own flesh and blood, and had not done all in her power, etc., etc.

'Indeed, aunt,' said Helen warmly, 'I know you have been as good to me as possible.'

But Mrs. Carlyon was of opinion that Helen's actions proved her to possess a very lukewarm gratitude for her kindness.

Helen gave no hint as to the reason which had really influenced her decision. She preferred any reproaches for wavering and playing fast and loose, to revealing the secret she had discovered. Her motives for this reticence were two. She hated the idea of being connected in the remotest way with anything disgraceful. She shuddered to think of being pointed out as the girl who had had a narrow escape of marrying a convict. She did not distinguish, as Beatrice did, between real guilt and outward shame; she was repelled and disgusted by the shame, and looked no further. Her liking for Fairfax withered up at the first chill shadow from the cloud which hung over him. Then it seemed to her dishonourable to tell another person's secret. She had no right to do so; it was no business of hers; and ordinary kindly feeling would have made her shrink from striking such a blow. So her silence remained unbroken.

Mr. Martin, meanwhile, was on the watch for the effect of his letter. He waited with malicious triumph to hear what had come of it, and as days passed and he only heard that the Carlyons had gone to London, and

the affair with Fairfax was off, he was
puzzled ; for nobody added a hint that
Fairfax had proved a shady character.
Some declared, indeed, that he had with-
drawn his suit ; others, who were of opinion
that Helen had refused him, freely expressed their sympathy with her aunt, who
was understood to be much disappointed
by this untoward turn of things. Mr.
Martin's bewilderment was increased by
Fairfax's continued stay in the place. He
waited anxiously to hear that he had taken
flight ; and when Fairfax still went about
as usual, the prolonged suspense and un-
certainty became very wearing, and had
an unfortunate effect on his temper.
The position of affairs perplexed him ; and
in taxing his imagination to account for it,
he went through more mental effort than he

had ever undergone before. He could not understand how Fairfax could remain in Cheynehurst ; and he looked forward to his departure with hope which he kept alive as long as he could, but which dwindled and finally went out.

It was clear that Mr. Martin's arrow had fallen harmless, and that whatever had broken off the affair between Fairfax and Helen, it was not his machinations.

It is provoking to exert yourself in a spirit of benevolence, and to fail in compassing your end ; but I fancy it must be more provoking to go out of your way to do a shabby thing to injure some one, and find that you have not succeeded. It must be painful to hurt one's conscience without any result, and to know that one's meanness was useless.

Mr. Martin's thrifty instincts made him
groan over the profitless piece of malice
he had been guilty of.   Such a deed ought
to bring in a large return to justify itself.

He never supposed that Helen had kept
silence about the letter.   Of course she had
shown it to her aunt and to Fairfax, whose
contempt of the accusation was shown by
his remaining on the spot.   He must have
proved to the Carlyons that there was no
foundation for it, and Helen must have
broken with him for some other reason.

Mr. Martin felt very nervous as he con-
structed this theory.   If the story was
false, it would be awkward—deuced awkward
—if the letter was traced to him.   With a
salutary fear of the consequences if its
authorship was detected, he firmly resolved
not to drop a word about Fairfax which

should lead anyone to suppose that he bore him a grudge, or did not hold him in high esteem. He would be very careful not to appear as his ill-wisher. It was the easier to do so, as the cause of his enmity was done away with. Fairfax, no longer a suitor of Helen Carlyon, he need not envy ; and as hope began to spring up that his own faithfulness might make him successful, emotions of almost Christian forbearance towards his quondam rival came to him.

Beatrice Clare was thinking of very much the same thing as Mr. Martin, certainly with very different feelings. She was expecting Fairfax's departure. Each day she looked for the call when he would say ' Good-bye.' Helen had told her that he wished to go away as soon as possible, and his rejection by Helen must add a spur to his desire. There was nothing to keep him now ; and as he delayed, she wished sometimes that he would go quickly, lest his secret should be published to the world. It was safe enough with Helen and herself ; but that anonymous letter, coming out of the dark, filled her with fear. The enemy who had done him that ill turn might do him another.

It was strange to see Fairfax and to talk to him about common things while her thoughts of him were so painful. But as he did not go, her nervous dread troubled her less. She got used to it, and Fairfax's continued stay reassured her somewhat.

He came often to the Vicarage, and she saw a good deal of him, and felt that he was grateful for the society that he got at their house, and that it cheered him. She was very glad that it was so, and she made his visits as pleasant as she could.

She never dreamt of being more than a friend to him : he loved Helen, and he could not turn to another directly, if there had been nothing else to come between them. She felt as the friends of a man who is dying feel—she must do all she could while she had the opportunity. It would be only for a short time that she could be anything to him ; and while she could lighten the shadow in which he dwelt, she would do it with reckless carelessness as to the future.

It was reckless ! She knew that she would pay a heavy reckoning for every hour he spent with her ; she would suffer for it in dulness and weariness when he went : but she would never again have the chance of gladdening him, and it could not be for long.   Though he lingered, he would go soon.

That was what Fairfax told himself when he was roused to ask what his object was in hanging about Cheynehurst.   He must go soon : meanwhile he would take what good he could get to sweeten his few last days. He stayed on simply because he could not go away.   There was no possible end to be gained by keeping within reach of Beatrice Clare.   She was divided from him by a gulf which would never be filled up.   He did not deceive himself for a second on that point.

But to be with her made him happy— with an imperfect, uneasy unhappiness which had a bitter after-taste, but which he could not deny himself.   Like Bee, he knew that he would pay a heavy reckoning for those days ; but he was something like a bankrupt who knows that he is ruined past redemption, and goes on increasing his liabilities.

He was just so far careful of the future that he believed he was only endangering his own peace. He was so well aware that he had no right to make love to Bee, that he felt sure of his own self control. He would never attempt to win anything but common friendliness from her—she was safe from him ; but he could not forego the brightness of her presence, and he went on blindly, putting off the end, which yet must come.

Each day when he could see her was a gain, something more with which to go through the ' years of cold ' which stretched before him when he lost her out of his life. He could not face them yet. They would come soon enough.

Presently he would find resolution to say farewell and leave her. It must be done before long, while she still thought well of him, before she heard his story. There was always the danger that it might come to her ears through some of her Middleton acquaintances, enough danger to make her neighbourhood unsafe for him.

It was well that he did not know where his real danger lay, and that his secret was in the possession of a man whose powers of ruling his tongue were not cultivated, and who, sooner or later, was pretty sure to relieve the dulness of existence in the country by publishing it.

CHAPTER XXIII.

'I became a reproof among all mine enemies, but especially among my neighbours : and they of mine acquaintance were afraid of me ; and they that did see me without conveyed themselves from me.'

Psalm xxxi. 13.

NE day, about the middle of February, Fairfax had occasion to drive into Stonehurst. The weather was very fine, and his spirits went up as he was carried rapidly through the crisp, clear air by a fast horse. He whistled snatches of airs, and talked cheerfully to Bob, who glowed with satisfaction at his master's mood.

When they entered the little town, Fairfax
pulled up at a shop he had to visit, and
jumped out, telling Bob to drive on to the
Sun, where they always put up.   He walked
into the shop—a saddler's—and began on
the business which had brought him.   It
was, in the first place, to complain of the
quality of some article which he had just
got there, and perhaps it was not surprising
that the shopkeeper resented his customer's
strictures, and replied in a lofty way to them.

'He was quite sure that when the thing
was sent it was in good condition; he
couldn't answer for what might have
happened to it since it had left his shop;
but he did know that he had sent one
exactly like it to Sir John Fanshawe's the
same day, and he had had no complaints
about that.'

'That has nothing to do with it,' said Fairfax, more amused than annoyed at the man's tone. 'The point is that what I got cannot be used, and I must return it.'

'I can't do that,' said Mr. Smith.

'You can't take it back?'

'Quite out of the question,' said Mr. Smith, shaking his head, and looking past his customer through the open door. Fairfax stared at him for a minute, amazed at the disappearance of his bland smile and eager desire to please. Then, with a slight shrug of his shoulders, he said:

'I want a riding-whip.'

Mr. Smith retired, and Fairfax, turning round from the counter, met the eyes of two shopmen fixed upon him with a rapt curiosity, which made him ask himself whether he had by any chance come out with something wrong in his dress. He faced towards the door, and as he stood waiting he heard some whispering behind his back.

Mr. Smith displayed what he had been asked for, and Fairfax chose what he wanted, the tradesman standing by and looking on with a severely neutral expression, as if he would not encourage any purchase. Fairfax wondered whether he had been drinking, and having made his selection, he was turning with a curt 'Good-morning,' when the man said rather nervously, yet firmly:

'If you could make it convenient to settle your account, sir—ours is a strictly ready-money business.'

'Your account? Why, you've never sent it in!' exclaimed Fairfax, divided between his first hypothesis that Mr. Smith's morning dram had been a large one, and a fancy that he was perhaps in money difficulties. The possibility of the latter being true made him add pleasantly: 'Certainly, I will pay it at once if you will make it out. I'll call as I come back; you can have it ready then.'

'It is ready,' said Mr. Smith hastily. 'I've got it here. I'll just add the money for this. It'll save your calling again, sir,' he added, with a touch of apology in his tone as he dipped a pen in the ink and drew a piece of paper towards him.

Mr. Smith was less profuse in his acknowledgments of payment than might have been expected from his style of giving thanks for an order. Fairfax walked out, wondering whether the poor fellow was in such straits that so small a sum was an object to him, and pitying him carelessly. He was not offended at being dunned, though he thought it a little odd when he remembered that Mr. Smith, having had to get him some article from London and not knowing its price, had asked him only ten days ago to wait till he could pay for everything. 'Perhaps a sudden call on him,' thought Fairfax, and dismissed the subject.

It was too bright a morning to think of bills. The wide street was gay with sunshine and moving figures; the bustle of market-day made the scene really picturesque. He sauntered towards the Sun, looking at the groups, looking half-consciously for a face he knew.

It was impossible to walk far in Stonehurst on market-day without meeting some acquaintance ; and presently Fairfax came face to face with a Major Charlton, a half-pay officer, who dwelt in the neighbourhood, and who had shown a cordial inclination to cultivate his society. He was going to hold out his hand with a smiling greeting, but the military man stared at him as if he were a stranger, and passed on. It seemed strange, but Fairfax disposed of it easily.

' He is short-sighted, and evidently did not recognise me.'

At the Sun he found his dog-cart drawn up just inside the gateway. The horse was in the shafts, eating a feed of corn, and Bob was standing near, looking disturbed.

' Why haven't you taken Waterwitch out ?' exclaimed Fairfax.

' I thought, sir '—Bob was painfully

confused—'that mebbe you wouldn't stay long, and—and it didn't seem worth while to take her out.'

' But I shall stay for at least two hours,' said Fairfax, rather impatiently. ' See to her, and then get something inside, Bob.'

' I don't care for anything, thank you, sir.'

' You must have a glass of beer.'

' Are you going in, sir ?'

The question seemed very superfluous.

' What's the matter ?' said Fairfax. ' You look quite pale. Aren't you well?'

' I do feel a bit upset, sir,' said Bob. ' If you wouldn't mind going back now, I'd take it kind.'

' Why, what can be the matter for you to give in like this ? Come in and get some brandy.'

'Oh, sir, please don't go in !' entreated Bob, in a whisper. ' There's—somebody—been telling lies about you.'

Fairfax started, and turned paler than Bob.

' You mean—the truth,' he said in a breathless way, as if he could barely utter the words.

Bob turned away and swore fiercely. There was no other adequate expression for his emotion.

' It's a shame,' he said huskily.

For a moment, the high walls surrounding the court seemed to waver before Fairfax's eyes, and the stones under his feet became insecure.

' Don't give way, sir,' said Bob. ' I was obliged to tell you—God forgive me for doing it ! If I hadn't, they would have told you inside. Come away. Never mind a pack of wicked lies!'

'I am going in,' said Fairfax quietly.

His wits had come back to him; he looked cool and steady; only a slight paleness and a little defiance in the carriage of his head told that he was not in an everyday mood. He walked into the house. He would see for himself how things were going; he would not be driven to flight by Bob's information. He would find out how he stood.

It was as good an opportunity as could have been found of feeling the pulse of popular feeling towards him. There were always a good many folks whom he knew to be met in the Sun on market-day. They lunched there in the course of their shopping; he had come now intending to order luncheon to be ready for himself in an hour.

He walked into the long coffee-room, feeling very little disturbance. One does not feel the effect of a blow at first, and Fairfax had not yet realized the full import of what he had heard.

He looked perfectly composed as he entered the room. Several of his acquaintances were there; and there was a perceptible pause in the talk as he appeared, which was enough to try his self-possession. The buzz stopped, and every eye was turned upon him with curiosity. Two or three yards from the door sat Mrs. Price. She turned her head away, and pushed back her skirt as he passed. As the skirt was walking-length, the action could only be regarded as symbolical, expressing the

reprobation which respectability awards to
disgrace. Next her was Mr. Hammond,
Fairfax's nearest neighbour, who looked at
him without giving any greeting, knitted
his grey eyebrows, and did all but say :
' How dare you show your face here ?' It
was the same with all the rest ; they cut
him dead.

He sat down at an empty table, and after
a time—a much longer time than he had
ever had to wait before — a waiter approached and took his order. Fairfax
could see some people near watching and
exchanging glances of surprise and disgust
at his audacity in ordering anything. He
asked for some wine and biscuits, and
taking up a newspaper he mechanically read
the advertisements, while he forced himself
to swallow half a biscuit and drink some

wine. It was poor enough sherry, but he did not notice the taste. His only active senses were sight and hearing ; he saw without looking the stares that were fastened on him ; he heard whispers which at another time could not have reached his ears.

' Shameful ! Such insolence to show himself among respectable people !'

' He looks quite unconcerned ! So hardened.'

' It must be true. He was evidently prepared ; he looked brazen when he came in !'

He sat through it as long as he could keep up an impassive appearance. At last he rose, and withdrew. As he passed out, he met a young man whose character did not stand very high in the neighbourhood.

He was extravagant and dissipated, and
given to low company; and his means
were not large enough to cause people to
excuse his way of life as the sowing of wild
oats.   Such indulgence is only extended to
young men whose fathers have well-filled
purses, and young North had not inherited
much from his father.

He was not a pleasant object as he
swaggered out of the bar.   He had the un-
wholesome look of a man who keeps late
irregular hours, and drinks steadily; his
clothes were in vulgar taste and untidily
put on; and his assured air made all his
defects more clearly visible.

Fairfax was barely on speaking terms
with him, and he was surprised to be ac-
costed in hail-fellow-well-met fashion.

'How d'you do, Fairfax?' he said, with

boisterous familiarity. 'Come into the bar and I'll stand you something. No? What's the hurry? When are you coming over to see me? I say, I wish you would. I've got a dog that I mean to back,' etc., etc.

Fairfax managed to shake him off, without showing any of the disgust he felt; but this patronizing notice humiliated him more deeply than the cold looks and dead cuts he had just received. Was this what was left for him—the society of such men as these? Did this low fellow look down upon him, and feel that his advances must be welcome?

As he issued from the door, he met a party coming in—Beatrice surrounded by her brothers. She was glowing with the fresh morning air, and looking pretty in

her plumy hat. She held out her hand
with the bright smile which made her face
charming.

'Oh, Mr. Fairfax, I am glad we have met
you——' she began ; then she stopped.

He was very pale ; he did not smile, and
he did not look her in the face. He took
off his hat and bowed formally ; he did
not touch her hand. He had no right
to the smallest sign of friendliness from
her.

Her hand fell by her side, and he saw it
with a sharp pang of regret. She would
never offer it to him again. Would she cut
him next time he met her ? She looked
at him with a startled dismay—a piteous,
wounded expression in her eyes ; and the
strangest sense of exultation rose within
him at this proof that his manner could

affect her, mingled with remorse that he had hurt her.

'Perhaps I could have made her care for me if I might have tried,' he thought.

He went on, passing the boys without a word; and hastily telling Bob to follow him with the dog-cart, he walked away. The sunshine was as bright as it had been when he came in; the street was as full; but he was only aware of a great desolation round him. He was shut in for ever by his disgrace.

CHAPTER XXIV.

'Now let it work. Mischief, thou art afoot.'

Julius Cæsar.

THE boys burst into a chorus of wonder and question at Fairfax's strange behaviour. Bee did not answer their remarks. She did not look surprised; she knew what had happened. She had expected it; but she felt stunned when the blow did fall.

She stood for a minute, looking after Fairfax as he strode away. Her heart ached for him; and she longed with a blind reckless passion to go with him, and show him that he had one friend to stand by him. She could have taken his part before all their little world; she would have been proud to stand at his side.

'Oh, if I were a man, I could do it,' she thought.

But, alas! she was a young woman, and she was more keenly conscious of her womanhood then than she had ever been. No man friend of Fairfax's could feel the rush of emotion which came over her—could feel that this sorrow was his as much as his friend's.

She took the boys in, preventing them from pestering Bob with questions; and in the hotel they quickly learnt what had taken place. Everyone there knew the Clares, and came to speak to Beatrice, eager to know whether she had heard this dreadful story about Mr. Fairfax. It gave an extra spice to the gossip to retail it to a person who knew him well.

There were already several stories, which it was impossible to harmonize; there were dark whispers that Mr. Fairfax had undergone a long term of penal servitude— 'herded with the lowest criminals,' said Mrs. Price impressively; hints that he had broken into a bank and robbed a·venerable relation, who had died of shame at the disgrace thus brought upon the family name; and it was generally declared that he had acquired his money in a dishonest way. This had been discovered; and he would shortly be stripped of his ill-gotten wealth, and maintained in a more modest way in one of her Majesty's prisons.

'They say,' said Mrs. Young, 'that he just got the property by fraud, and that he will have to give it up. The real heirs have discovered the cheat, and they are determined to prosecute him. He went down on his knees to them, and offered to give up everything if they wouldn't expose him; but they were firm.'

'No, no,' said her husband, who had the graceful habit of setting his wife right in public; 'you're wrong, Fanny. It was his grandfather, whom he robbed years ago, that he went down on his knees to. He stole from the old man's safe, Miss Clare. I heard nothing about the way he got his property.'

'Oh, but, indeed, half a dozen people told me!' cried Mrs. Young.

'Yes, Mr. Young; Mr. Norton, the

lawyer, told me so,' said Mrs. Price. 'He said that now his fraud is discovered, Mr. Fairfax would run away; but he is watched by detectives. He may be arrested any minute.'

'Fancy anything so dreadful!' said Mrs. Young, with much relish. 'A man that you've met in society being arrested! I wonder how he can sleep!'

'The fellow is a regular swindler—a man of no character at all. It is a crying shame that such a person should dare to associate with us,' said Mr. Hammond.

'I never liked him,' said Mr. Martin complacently. 'I always thought there was something fishy about him.'

'There was certainly something very peculiar about him,' said Mr. Young. 'One sees it when one looks back.

He always appeared to wish to avoid one.'

'I suppose he just came here to raise as much money as he could,' said Mr. Hammond. 'Probably he saw the game would be up soon, and wanted to lay hands on what he could get. He has been raising money most recklessly, I understand — selling timber.'

'Perfectly stripped the land—it is quite bare,' Mrs. Price took up the tale. 'The man who ought to have it cried when he saw the state of things, and said there wouldn't be a stick left for him.'

'Oh, that's rot!' burst out Archie. 'He hasn't cut many trees in the park—I know better.'

'Hush, Archie!' said Bee mechanically, while Mrs. Price looked a rebuke.

'You should show more respect for your elders, Master Archie,' said Mr. Hammond good-naturedly.

Archie coloured, but the frank blue eyes did not fall.

'I beg your pardon; I didn't mean to be rude,' he said. 'But somebody's been telling a cram about Mr. Fairfax and the wood. I know he has sold very little. You can see for yourselves in the park— it isn't bare.'

'No, it isn't,' said Eustace, while a murmur from Alf supported the same assertion.

'The trees will be cut, I fear,' said Mr. Hammond.

'I heard they were all sold,' said Mrs. Young; 'and they say, too, that he has got frightfully into debt. He has run up bills right and left, and now that he is losing his property nobody will be paid. That is shocking for the poor shop-keepers.'

'Old Smith — I was in his shop this morning,' said Mr. Martin, 'and he was in a precious funk. Said he had never seen a penny of Mr. Fairfax's money— didn't believe he ever would; but he swore he would put it into the County Court.'

'It will be very hard on the poor fellows to lose their money,' said Mr. Hammond, 'and there's little chance of their being paid, if it is true that a notice has been served on all the tenants not to pay rent to this man.'

Mr. Young whistled under his breath.

'There must be some truth in the story about the way he got the property, then.'

'Oh, there's no doubt of it!' said Mrs. Price.

'But I should think the people he has got things from will be paid out of the estate,' said Mr. Young, remembering that he had sold Fairfax some hay a day or two ago, and charged him, as an acquaintance, a price which he could not have put on it in the open market. 'Surely it is only fair that they should be. They supplied the establishment at the Manor, and the master, whoever he may turn out to be, should be liable. Don't you think so, Mr. Hammond?'

Mr. Hammond shook his head, as who should say he took a less superficial view than the person who addressed him.

'They'll have to wait a precious time before they get paid, at that rate,' said

Mr. Martin. 'I would rather get my money now, and if he's been raising coin he ought to fork out honestly.'

'Honestly!' cried Mrs. Young. 'You may be sure the last thing he will intend is to be honest.'

Mr. Young fell silent, deeply occupied with the severe mental labour of drawing up a form of letter which should wring payment from his slippery debtor. Composition — except of the most ordinary business notes—being an unusual exercise to him, it was not easy to frame sentences which should intimate that Mr. Young was not a person to be trifled with, and that for Mr. Fairfax's own peace of mind he would find it advisable to settle the debt at once.

Bee had said very little so far, as little

as in common courtesy she could. She
had no voice, the painful swelling in her
throat choked her; and at first she dreaded
to show too much indignation. She let
them talk, thinking it wise to hear all
there was to hear ; and by degrees she grew
calmer, almost relieved, as it became evident
that the tongues of the scandal-mongers
had run beyond fact and left it very far
behind. They were welcome to heap any
opprobrium on his head, provided they did
not touch upon his real trouble.

She put a strong guard upon herself, and
managed to look fairly unconcerned ; trying to smile and not let the fear which
chilled her heart look out of her eyes.
When they got to the woes of the unpaid
tradespeople, she was cool enough to say
carelessly :

'How can you believe such absurd stories? Is it likely that Mr. Fairfax would have the property for four years if there was anything wrong? And how could he get it dishonestly?'

'They say he forged the will,' said Mrs. Price.

'Oh, no! I heard that he is not really a Fairfax at all. His real name is—dear me, what did I hear it was? I forget,' said Mrs. Young; 'but anyway, he isn't a Fairfax. He is a claimant, you know, like that Tichborne; he has imposed upon people, and now it is found out. It is quite romantic.'

'It's all nonsense!' cried Bee impetuously, contradicting the story the more eagerly because she was glad that she could do so. 'The whole story is absurd on the face of it, and quite impossible. I would wait till there is something more than that to go upon.'

'Well, there must be something in it,' said Mrs. Price, 'or else how did people get hold of it?'

'There is no smoke without fire,' added Mr. Hammond. 'Of course, my dear Miss Clare, as Mr. Fairfax is a friend of your father's, you will be incredulous about this.'

'Of course,' said Bee curtly.

'No doubt all the reports cannot be true,' went on Mr. Hammond, in a tone of judicial moderation, 'and some are very much exaggerated. These things always are, and one must make allowance for that. But they cannot all be false either. There must be a foundation for some of them.'

'He mayn't have been so long in prison as people say,' observed Mrs. Price ; 'but he must have been there for a time.'

'I believe there is no doubt of that,' said Mr. Martin.

'What evidence is there for it ? What have you heard?' asked Bee, turning to him.

The point-blank question seemed to take him by surprise. He looked confused, and did not meet steadily the keen glance of her eyes. Tall and broad fellow as he was, he shrank before her, and mumbled in reply that everybody said so. He was not going to give the real authority, or to assume the responsibility of beginning the talk.

'If that is all the evidence you have, I would not be so ready to believe such a story, or to repeat it,' said Bee. 'Have you finished, Alf ?' she added abruptly.

Alfred replied that he had, and she rose hastily, and drew on her gloves, fastening them a little more deliberately than usual because her fingers were trembling.

'It is quite shocking,' said Mrs. Price, 'to think that your brothers have been so much with Mr. Fairfax. I hope that they've taken no harm ; but boys are so easily led, and evil communications——'

Bee laughed, and Archie and Eustace broke out together :

'It's all crams about Mr. Fairfax ! He couldn't go to gaol ! He is a gentleman !'

'And he's awfully good,' added Eustace solus, with a hostile glance at Mr. Martin. , He never misses church.'

This was a home-thrust, for Mr. Martin was not so regular in his attendance at church as could be desired.

'I think,' said Bee gravely, 'that my father is a good judge of the persons the boys associate with.'

She said good-morning to her friends and departed. She had not finished her business in the town, and she did all she had intended to do as methodically and carefully as usual. She could not act as though she felt more than a sympathy which did not disable her for common work; she had no right to yield to regret. His trouble was nothing personal to her.

She drove home late in the afternoon in her little pony-carriage; the boys pressing up close to her, trampling on her dress and feet, and all talking together in a white heat of indignation at the people who said such wicked things of their friend.

'You'll tell papa, Bee?' they urged, as they reached the house.

'Yes, I suppose I must,' she said heavily.

'Would you rather not? I'll tell him if you like,' cried Eustace.

'No, no,' said Bee, rather sharply. 'I will tell him.'

Mr. Clare was not in, the servant said; he had gone out a little while ago. 'Mrs. Price was here to see him, and Mr. Hammond came after her.'

'Then I need not tell him,' said Bee to herself. 'He will have heard it all.'

CHAPTER XXV.

'I NEVER heard such nonsense in my life,' said Mr. Clare scornfully.

Mrs. Price, who had felt it her duty to tell him the tales afloat about Mr. Fairfax, took this remark with lofty magnanimity. She looked at Mr. Clare as he spoke with decided uncivility, and nodded calmly.

'I assure you, Mr. Clare, I heard all this. I hope it is nonsense; but I fear——'

'Of course it is nonsense,' said Mr. Clare,

so bewildered that he clung to that assertion as a stay.

'Saying it is nonsense doesn't prove that
it is.'

'But, my dear Mrs. Price, is it worth
while to prove that such wild slanders are
false?   I am surprised that you should
listen to them.   On the face of them, they
are impossible.'

'I don't quite see that.   There is no
smoke without fire.'   Mrs. Price nodded
again, and looked provokingly cool and
decidedly of her own opinion.   'I came to
tell you because, as you have been friendly
to this unfortunate young man, you ought
to know what a very doubtful person he
turns out to be.'

'I am not aware that he has turned out
anything,' said Mr. Clare sharply.   'I

shall certainly not doubt him on such grounds as the mass of scandal you have been kind enough to bring me.'

It was useless to strike at Mrs. Price in this way. Such blows glided off her self-complacency.

'Of course I felt obliged to tell you, Mr. Clare,' she said. 'In your position as the clergyman of the parish, you should know such things, and it would be wrong not to let you know what is said about him.

'This unfortunate young man, as you are pleased to call him, is my friend as well as my parishioner, Mrs. Price.'

'Exactly. That made me more anxious that you should not remain in ignorance about him. It would never do for you to have him at your house while such a stain rests upon his character.'

43—2

' A stain !' cried Mr. Clare. ' You have accused him of half a dozen things—you have blackened his character all over.'

' I beg your pardon. I have not accused him at all: I have simply repeated what others have said.'

' It comes pretty much to the same thing. Who told you these stories ? Who is the authority for them ?'

There was no getting a definite answer on that point. Mrs. Price could give no authority. The stories had one of the marks which justify the acceptance of tradition—they were told by everybody; but who the first teller was was unknown.

Mr. Clare was left in a very bad temper when Mrs. Price departed. He felt keenly the annoyance of being disturbed in the enjoyment of a quiet afternoon. It was bad to have his leisure-time spoilt, and it was worse to have it done by a call from Mrs. Price, whom he hated as heartily as a clergyman ever allows himself to hate a parishioner. He was annoyed by her gossip, but it made little impression on him; he set it down as women's exaggeration, and dismissed it from his mind as soon as Mrs. Price relieved him from her presence, and went back to his book with a sensation of relief.

Some ten minutes after, Mr. Hammond was announced. Mr. Clare put down his book with a stifled groan. He had been making ungallant mental comments upon women's talk; but he did not feel that a man's talk would be much more enjoy-

able.   Mr. Hammond was garrulous ; it
was a peculiarly provoking chance that he
should succeed Mrs. Price.

Mr. Hammond had come to tell pretty
much the same tale as Mrs. Price had
poured   forth.   Mr.   Clare   treated   his
account more respectfully ; indeed, he was
gravely disturbed by it.   The statements
which in Mrs. Price's mouth were exaggerations, were taken more seriously now.
Mr. Clare still protested that it was all
nonsense ; but he was made uncomfortable
by the nonsense.   He did not believe a
word ;   but it was awkward that such
scandals were abroad, and had gained
general acceptance.   When Mr. Hammond
had gone, Mr. Clare set off to the Manor
House.   He could not settle again that
afternoon, and he felt a kindly wish to

see Fairfax, after the description he had heard of the way in which he had been cut.

Measures must be taken to put down the slanders as quickly as might be. Mr. Clare knew well enough how difficult it is to put an end to a report against a man's character, when once it has been credited ; and he was anxious to crush the life out of these reports at once.

People, as a rule, enjoy believing ill of their neighbours. Tell an acquaintance that Mr. Smith has given ten thousand pounds to a hospital, and the chances are that he will reply, 'That can't be true. Smith hasn't the money, and he's too stingy to give it away if he had.' Tell him that the same Smith has taken ship for Spain, after carrying out a series

of audacious frauds, and he will probably
exclaim, ' Really ?   How much has he gone
off with ?'

Mr. Clare was shown into the library.
Fairfax was there, sitting by the fire.   He
rose as his visitor entered, but he did
not speak or come forward.   His face
was pale and drawn, and there was
an almost sullen expression on it, as if
he expected nothing pleasant from the
interview, and steeled himself to endure
whatever he might have to bear.   This
look and his silence gave Mr. Clare a
positive shock.   It was dreadful to see
that blank, resolute calmness ; it was as
if the young man acknowledged his right
to judge him, and bent before it ; he felt
almost humiliated to see such a look on
the face of a man who had been his

equal till to-day. He stopped short, and there was a silence as they regarded each other; then Fairfax half turned away.

'You have heard,' he said.

'My dear fellow——' began Mr. Clare, and paused, for he did not know what to say.

'And you have come at once.'

'Of course I came to see you. Won't you ask me to sit down?' said Mr. Clare, taking a chair.

Fairfax remained standing. He rested his arm on the mantelpiece, and he looked his visitor straight in the face.

'It is kind of you,' he said quietly. 'You wished to ask me whether it is true —you would not turn away from me at once.'

'I did not come on any such errand,' said Mr. Clare bluntly. 'I felt sure it was all false. It must be false. It is very unpleasant for you that people have taken to using their powers of invention so unjustifiably about you; but you must not let such nonsense upset you.'

Spite of Fairfax's dejection, it seemed impossible that there should be any grain of truth in the reports. The clear-cut, refined face, the thoughtful steady eyes, gave the lie to them.

'It is not false,' said Fairfax briefly.

Mr. Clare gazed at him in utter amazement for a few seconds.

'What is not false?' he said at last. 'I have heard half a dozen stories about you. We are playing at cross purposes,' he added eagerly, catching at an obvious explanation.

Some old scrape of Fairfax's had been dragged out of the decent obscurity to which it should be consigned, and he was suffering on that account. He was just the man who could repent thoroughly of youthful misconduct.

'You refer to one thing, and I refer to another. It is false, I suppose, that you have had five years' penal servitude?'

Mr. Clare put the question with a laugh. Fairfax walked away to the window, and answered in a hollow voice:

'I have had a year's hard labour.'

There was another silence. Mr. Clare was stunned. This was as bad as the worst thing he had heard.

Fairfax made no attempt to soften down the fact. He stated it as bluntly and harshly as possible; and having spoken, stood looking out through the window, seeing, not the green slopes of the park, but the wide road into which he had walked from the prison-door, the flood of sunshine, and a girl's face and figure. The thing he had told had never been so hideous to him as it was then.

' Good heavens!' exclaimed Mr. Clare at last. ' Are you in earnest?'

' It isn't a subject to joke about,' said Fairfax.

' Well?' said Mr. Clare sharply.

' I beg your pardon?'

The tone of his voice affected Mr. Clare's nerves unpleasantly. It told of hopeless dreariness and accepted despair. It was not natural for a young voice to speak in that listless, dejected way.

' Well? Haven't you anything more to

say to me? Is that all you choose to say about it?'

'That is enough, isn't it? The other stories you have heard are not true.'

'I don't mean that. Surely you have more to say to me. We are friends, Fairfax. There must be some explanation of this terrible thing.'

'I have no explanation to give,' he said, in the same monotonous tone. 'The thing is there—nothing can alter it. But there is one thing I should like to say — I ought not to have let you make a friend of me. I am sorry that I accepted your friendship on false pretences. It was wrong.'

'Can't you say that you suffered unjustly?' said Mr. Clare.

Fairfax faced round quickly.

'What use is it to say so?' he cried, almost angrily. 'Who would believe me? Every knave can tell that story.'

'You were innocent, then. Come, Fairfax, you are very sore and angry with the world; but you needn't treat me as a representative of it. I need not ask—I am sure you were innocent.'

'I was,' said Fairfax curtly.

Mr. Clare made an inarticulate sound of sympathy, and furtively applied his handkerchief to his eyes.

'You might have known that I should feel confidence in you,' he said reproachfully. 'The idea of taking it for granted that I should believe you had deserved such a thing!'

'When one has been branded one doesn't get rid of the feel of it. And you have

only my word to go upon—the evidence
went the other way.'

'Evidence isn't gospel,' said Mr. Clare.
'I prefer your word.'

Fairfax looked at him gratefully, and
Mr. Clare's perceptions were not keen
enough to see that under his gratitude
he winced. He had said just before that
he would not be believed; but it gave him
more pain than satisfaction to be assured
that his word was credited. He felt, in
the blind irritation of suffering, that it was
bitter that he had to be grateful for such
an assurance. He was so wretched that
the kindliest intentions hurt him. He was
touched by Mr. Clare's friendliness, and
thankful for it—yet it wounded him.

'It is a sad thing,' went on Mr. Clare,
feeling it incumbent on him to try to

console, and conscious of an absolute want
of any material to produce consolation from
—'a terrible misfortune; but you must not
take it too much to heart. So long as your
conscience is clear——'

Fairfax half smiled with a dreary bitterness, and Mr. Clare stopped. His remarks
had a feeble sound which did not encourage
him to continue them.

'I doubt whether my clear conscience
does me much good. It doesn't mitigate
the penalty. I am disgraced as surely as
if I had done the thing.'

'But you must have more courage to
bear it when you know that it is unde-
served,' urged Mr. Clare.

'Do you think so?'

'I am sure you think so yourself. It
must help you.'

'One always hears that said, and I suppose I ought to feel it,' said Fairfax. 'And no doubt, for one's own self-respect, it is better to know that one is innocent. But there is another side to it. If I had been guilty, I should at least know that I had been fairly treated. The feeling that one has suffered unjustly is as bitter as anything can be. It eats into one like a canker, and assurance of one's own integrity only makes one resent it more deeply. You don't know what disgrace is—nobody can know who has not felt it—it stirs up evil in one. You talk of bearing as if it were an ordinary trouble. But what fortitude can I find to bear vulgar, public disgrace patiently? I am simply ruined—damned for life, and all for no good—no reason.'

'No no; you are exaggerating, Fairfax. You will live it down.'

'In how many years, I wonder? No; if I lived for a century it would always be remembered that I had been a common felon. The utmost I can expect is to be considered a " reformed character," who may relapse at any moment into his evil ways.'

He was walking up and down the room, and he took a few turns in silence after that. Mr. Clare did not disturb him; this case was beyond his powers. Trite commonplaces could not touch it. He felt as if Fairfax were older than himself, aged by this dismal knowledge, this fiery ordeal; and like Job's friends he said no word, for he saw his sorrow was very great.

Presently Fairfax stopped walking, and sat down.

'There is no need to inflict my troubles on you,' he said quietly. 'You are very kind, and I am making a bad return for it. But I cannot talk calmly of the affair even now.'

'I understand.'

'I am glad that you have not cast me off; it is something to be believed in.'

'Nobody that knows you can believe in the story—at least that you were to blame,' said Mr. Clare, exaggerating in the warmth of the moment.

Fairfax took the speech at what it was worth, and was not tempted for a moment to expect that his acquaintances would show faith in him.

' You will prove that it is false yet,
said Mr. Clare. ' I must go now, but
I shall see you again. By the way—I
quite forgot—aren't you coming to dine
with us this evening ?'

' I was,' said Fairfax ; ' but,' and he
drew his head up with a touch of defiant
pride, ' it is different now.'

' Nonsense !' cried Mr. Clare. ' You
aren't going to shut yourself up and brood
at home. What difference is there ? Show
people that you aren't ashamed, having
nothing to be ashamed of. Come to the
Vicarage—we shall expect you. There
will be only ourselves, so you won't be
teased by strangers.'

Mr. Clare took his way homewards,
in much perturbation of spirit, and went
to talk over with his daughter the incredible

thing which he had heard. He did not find her able to share his bewilderment. He was yet more surprised when Bee told him that she knew Fairfax's secret; she had known it for six weeks.

'I could not tell you, papa,' she said apologetically. 'I hated to speak of it, and I knew he was not going to live here. Was it wrong to keep it back from you?'

Mr. Clare did not pronounce any decision on this point.

'It was very natural that you should dislike repeating such a story,' he said.

Perhaps, he reflected afterwards, it was just as well that Bee had kept her information to herself. If she had told him, it would have put him into an awkward

position with Fairfax. He could scarcely
have avoided making some inquiry into the
facts, and he would have heartily disliked
doing so.

When the evening came, Fairfax presented himself at the Vicarage. A curious
impulse drove him to seek Beatrice Clare's
presence. He wanted to show her that
he could face her eyes even in this position;
and this feeling was so strong that it
overcame his shrinking from the kindness
which he was sure she would give him.
She would be sorry for him, and she would
show her sympathy with all the tact which
a woman could exercise; and to him, in
the captiousness of his suffering, her kindness would be as sweet as vinegar mingled
with gall.

But at least, if he was not to be cast

off as a friend, if he was still to be admitted to her acquaintance, he would bear the awkwardness of the position like a man, with such spirit as he could show. He would not play the part of an unfortunate person, a mendicant for her pity. She should not think of him as hiding himself. He would have as much of her respect as he could gain in his fallen estate. This feeling of defiance gave a sternness to his gravity as he entered the Vicarage, which caused the man who admitted him, and helped him as respectfully as ever off with his greatcoat, to remark afterwards that there must be some mistake about Mr. Fairfax—he looked more like a man who was proud of himself than ashamed.

Self-possessed as he looked, the moment when he walked into the drawing-room was perhaps the hardest of that hard day. It taxed his power of endurance to its utmost limit to see her, knowing that she knew his secret. He could bear Mr. Clare's kindness, but to be condemned to considerate kindness and tact from Bee, was what he could not bear.

She greeted him just as usual; there was nothing in her manner to remind him that he was on a different footing now. She felt too shy to make any sign of sympathy.

As they stood round the fire before dinner was announced, she chatted so lightly and easily that it gave Fairfax an odd sense of unreality. Nothing seemed changed. Her very dress was perfectly familiar to him; he had seen her wearing it several times: all the surroundings he had learnt by heart. Could it be possible that everything was changed for him now?

Bee remained serenely self-possessed during dinner. She exerted herself to keep up conversation, and Fairfax seconded her —now and then with a grudging inquiry in his heart whether she cared so little that the event which marked out the day did not disturb her equanimity much. Well, why should she trouble herself about it? She had no share in the matter. He had come dreading her pity, her soft looks or speech of sympathy; and his fears had been superfluous. She took the business easily enough, as she might have done if the curate, say, had fallen into trouble. Fairfax was a very recent acquaintance— why should she care? It was much better

that she did not.   He was glad to escape
condolences, but yet once or twice he
wondered whether she was as indifferent
as she looked.   And with average human
consistency, finding that he was not to
endure condolences, he began to think that
they would have been desirable.

Mr. Clare did not appear so much at
ease as his daughter did.   He looked
subdued and did not talk much; he was
in fact nervously anxious to comport himself suitably, and to do and say nothing
which could hurt Fairfax's feelings.   His
head was full of his friend's misfortune, and
he was unable to make a pretence of cheerful unconsciousness.

Long before the dinner was over, he
was of opinion that he had done un-
wisely in persuading Fairfax to come; it

would have been better to leave him to the healing influences of solitude. Talk must be a mockery to the poor fellow, and yet one must talk to him.

When Bee had left them, Mr. Clare allowed his facial muscles to droop as his heart dictated, mournfully pushed the claret-jug over to Fairfax, and relapsed into silence.

' Fairfax,' he said at last, ' will you let me ask you a question? This happened to you before you got your money, I suppose?'

Fairfax nodded.

' Did you make any attempt to discover the real state of the case afterwards?'

' I set a detective to work, but he did nothing.'

' Can't anything be done ?'

Fairfax made a restless movement.

' No ; I see no chance of it. I have done all I could. You don't suppose that a man sits down tamely under such a load, and doesn't try every means to get rid of it.'

' No, no ; of course not. I was wonder- ing whether in time you might hope to pick up evidence that would clear you.'

Fairfax shook his head.

' I have no hope left,' he said. ' In fact, I dare not think of it.'

' Time does a great deal,' said Mr. Clare. ' I would put my trust in it if I were you.'

' Time doesn't work miracles, and nothing short of a miracle can do me any good.'

He was silent for a few minutes; then he got up.

'I think, if you will excuse me, I will say good-night, Mr. Clare. It is early, but I am very bad company to-night, and you have borne quite enough of my dolefulness already.'

'No, no. I am very glad you came.'

'Thank you. Good-night.'

He said nothing about Beatrice. Mr. Clare supposed that the poor fellow had forgotten anything so irrelevant to his private griefs, little guessing that it was Bee herself who gave the keenest edge to his misfortunes, that it was she who filled Fairfax's thoughts as he went away.

It was a mistake to go near her again. He had been most ludicrously wrong about her altogether. He had braced himself to endure and tacitly refuse her pity; and she treated him as if she thought nothing of his trouble, and gave it only a careless passing consideration. He had not been very presumptuous in his expectations; he had only supposed that she would take such a share as anyone whom a man calls friend may take in his affairs, and that she would find a way of saying: 'I am sorry.'

He would have repelled any such demonstration, for the last person whom a proud man can receive pity from is the woman he loves; but when he was not called upon to repel it, he felt wounded.

She need not have preserved such a strict silence, or at least she might have shown sympathy by voice and manner. It was

quite true that the blight which had be-
fallen him was best unnoticed, but he did
not like her to treat it so. It seemed to
make his shadow of disgrace blacker, as a
pointed overlooking of any defect in one's
appearance makes one nervously conscious
of it.

Was it a horrified sense of his degradation which made her entrench herself in
silence? Perhaps she shrank from him
now in dainty disgust, and wished to keep
him at a suitable distance. He was scarcely
a proper acquaintance for her, and she
would be keenly susceptible to that—more
susceptible than her father; for women are
so conventional, thought Fairfax, falling
into the fatally facile commonplaces which
are always ready to supply the want of
observation. They looked at the outside

with most attention, and she might very reasonably object to intimacy with a man who was under a cloud for life.

She would be kind from a distance, but she could not feel real sympathy for his fallen condition; it must revolt her, and it had been irrational to suppose that she could stoop near enough to feel hearty human compassion for him. She would be sorry, with a shiver of disgust at having such unpleasant realities forced upon her notice; she would throw him a ' Poor fellow,' and shake hands with an effort.

Fairfax remembered her as she had been that night: her evident determination to ignore what she had heard about him, her careful choice of topics which could be discussed with any stranger, and should not come too near what had happened that day; and some fierce incoherent words trembled on his lips. The fierceness was not against her—how could she help it? What comprehension could she have in her sheltered days for a lot like his?

It was much that she gave him charity —cold as the proverbial virtue—that she did not think his stigma banished him entirely from the outer circle of her acquaintance.

But he would not trespass too far on her kindness. It had been a mistake to go that evening. His imagination of her would have been sweeter than the reality; the gentle compassion he had dreaded would have been pleasanter to dwell on than her smiling indifference.

So he tormented himself with remembrance of her words and looks, making them mean all that could fret and wound him most; and in his dreams that night, in which all the painful scenes of the day were repeated, he saw most distinctly, and with most pain, Bee's face in its smiling society calm turned to him. All the bitterness of his case was summed up and expressed in that — the irremediable loss, the loneliness, the cruel anguish of separateness.

' Has Mr. Fairfax gone, papa ?' said Bee, when her father joined her.

' Yes; he seemed anxious to get away. I dare say he will feel better alone.'

' Very likely.'

' It is awkward having him when he has so much on his mind,' said Mr. Clare. ' I thought it kinder to persuade him to come,

but it doesn't seem a happy idea to me
now. We all felt the awkwardness of it.
I think even your tact failed, Bee. You
were too determined to talk as if nothing
had happened.'

Bee started and flushed hotly.

' Did — did Mr. Fairfax——' she said
quickly.

' My dear child, how could he say anything about it ? He never mentioned you.
But I fancy he was rather oppressed by
your remarks.'

' I thought it would be the best way
to ignore — what we heard,' said Bee
briefly.

' Perhaps you are right,' rejoined Mr.
Clare.

He took up a book, and Bee went on
with a piece of work.

'Papa,' she said suddenly, 'did it seem very unfeeling?'

Mr. Clare raised his eyes with an expression of mild perplexity.

'Would he think me unfriendly to rattle on as I did to-night? Did it sound very shallow and frivolous?'

'No, no, Bee—you are taking it too seriously. You did not rattle, dear; I only fancied that Fairfax was not inclined to discuss the news of the day as fully as you chose to do. I dare say though, in one way, he would be glad to see that you made no difference in your manner to him,' said Mr. Clare reassuringly.

Bee winced. It was cruel to think of his caring about people's manner, being glad that they made no difference.

'Did I hurt him?' she asked herself.

'Did I vex him again with my stupid chatter? But I did not know what to do. I was afraid to show I was sorry. I must try to manage better next time I see him.'

CHAPTER XXVI.

'I only fly
Your looks because they stir
Griefs that should sleep.'

SHELLEY.

UT the next time was longer in coming than Bee expected. She had seen so much of Fairfax lately that she instinctively looked for his frequent visits; and it seemed as if, in the present state of things, they must see him oftener. Her father would take pains to be with him and prevent him from brood-

ing, and she would have abundant oppor-
tunities of showing him kindness.

But she was wrong. Fairfax came little
to the Vicarage, and he came apparently
only to see Mr. Clare. They sat together
in the study, and Bee heard afterwards
that he had been in the house. After
two or three of these calls, it dawned
upon her that Fairfax was avoiding her
purposely. Nothing but deliberate intention on his part could account for his
not seeing her. She grieved over this,
but without any sense of personal injury.
She thought that he shrank morbidly
from society, and found it unbearable.
Her father was the only person with
whom he was intimate enough to find
relief in his company.

It was quite natural, but she grew

very sad as she was made to give up her faint hope of doing him friendly offices, and her utter impotence was forced upon her. She could not give him a drop of comfort; she could only think of him as the days passed, seeing how wearily they must drag for him, wondering how he was bearing his burden. It would have been impossible not to think of him constantly, even if she had only felt ordinary friendship for him. He was kept before her mind not only by his incurable trouble, but by the talk she heard.

There was a stir of excitement in Cheynehurst, and a stream of callers came to the Vicarage to discuss the subject thoroughly. It was talked threadbare in that drawing-room; talked over till the mere sound of the name of Fairfax made Bee's heart beat nervously; talked over till she was sick of the effort of restraining herself so far as to answer quietly.

She heard all the stories, which grew to romantic height, all the exaggerations, all the slanders; and she had to sit still and listen and answer with polite calm, as if she cared nothing, as though every word spoken against him did not hurt her as if it had touched a nerve.

It was a positive torture of her heart and feelings which she had to undergo, and she went through it with unflinching spirit; never betraying what her suffering was, nor letting any feeling of hers prevent her from doing what a friend could to clear him. She stood up for him frankly

and openly, defended him from every false
accusation, contradicted all the exaggerations and the untrue statements that she
heard, and took his part manfully in every
way that was possible. But she was
obliged to admit the truth; and she grew
—oh, so tired of saying 'That is true,'
when the crucial question was put; so
painfully weary of listening in silence to
the expressions of contempt for him which
followed.

A weak woman or a cowardly woman
would have been quickly cured of any
liking for a man in such a position; but
Bee had an obstinate strength in her, and
the storm of popular disfavour only made
her cling the closer to him. There are
some women who love most passionately
when the man they care for is at some

disadvantage, and there is no worldly credit or honour to be gained by association with him; and Bee was one of them.

The good people of Cheynehurst did Fairfax yeoman's service then with the best intentions to do him none. If there had been a chance of Bee recovering from the impression he had made upon her, they destroyed it completely. He was held up continually to her pity, and she was forced into the position of his champion; it was only natural that any liking which she had for him should be strengthened and ripened.

Indeed, if she had only cared for him as an acquaintance, the instinct of a generous nature would have made her take his part. Because others turned away, there was the more need that he should keep what friends he could. She believed in him, it is necessary to repeat; and therefore it was easy to be faithful to him.

But she found it useless to repeat Fairfax's disclaimer of guilt. Of course he said so; people were always innocent if you believed their story; but Cheyne-hurst was worldly-wise. Bee began to think it very difficult to love her neighbour as a good Christian should, when her neighbour showed himself or herself uncharitable and fond of evil reports.

One afternoon, after a severe attack of callers, she rushed out of the house when the sixth had gone, feeling that she could endure no more assurances that the speaker had always thought there was something

strange and not quite nice about Mr.
Fairfax, nor expressions of wonder that
Mr. Clare would allow such a person to
cross his threshold. She threw on her
hat and cloak, and went out at the side-
door, to escape any callers who might be
advancing by the high-road. She went
through the garden and orchard, and struck
into a field path which she was pretty sure
to have to herself.

It was a mild day in March, and the
air was soft and pleasant; but Bee was
too worried to be soothed by it. She
was full of angry disgust, sickened with
the vulgar pleasure in misfortune and evil
which she had been witnessing, revolted
by the complacency with which people,
whom she had formerly thought kind-
hearted, gloated over every detail of the

painful story.   It was a shock to receive
such thorough lessons in the failings of
human nature.

' They all fall upon him in their hearts
and worry him; they are glad to say
harsh things of him and think of his
humiliation and pain,' she thought, with
a sob in her throat. ' Are we all cruel
by nature ?   Should I talk as they do
if I didn't care for him?   Could I ever
be hard enough to think a man's wrecked
life a pleasant subject for chatter, and
pour out " Ohs !" and " Ahs !" and
" Shockings !" over it, and never feel a
bit of compunction ?   I hope not.   I should
be sorry, I think, for my enemy if I had
one, and I knew that his character was
thrown to the vultures in this way.   I
think—I hope I should have a good word

for anybody who was so beset. And *he* knows how they are talking; he told papa that he didn't expect to be believed· How he must hate the whole world !'

She was hurrying along when she saw Fairfax at a little distance, walking over the field towards her. She instinctively slackened her pace and tried to appear quite composed, becoming aware that she must look disturbed and agitated. She could not help being glad that he was so thrown in her way that he was forced to speak to her; she was not reconciled to being set aside as one of the world which he must hate, and she could not quite give up a hope that she might find a way which could not wound him of showing him that her friendship was not affected. She walked on sedately, blessing the chance that had brought her this way.

A few feet from the point where they must meet, a path crossed the one in which they were walking.

Fairfax turned into the cross-way, raising his hat with a courteous, formal bow, which Bee had scarcely presence of mind enough to return, she was so taken by surprise. She gazed at his retreating figure in blank astonishment. What had she done? Did he mean to forswear all his acquaintances here? But he had not given her father up, and why must he turn on her because other people were blind and unjust?

She was a little paler than before as she walked on. The muscles about her lips were firmly set; she had forgotten her sympathetic mood of a minute ago, and the good excuses which she had made for his avoidance of her, and she was angry with him. He had no right—no right to decline her acquaintance, and if he was not very stupid he must know that he had behaved in a way to wound her. 'For we used to be friends, and he ought not to forget that. Because he is very unhappy and ill-treated, it doesn't excuse him for being hard to me.'

She crossed the stile, and was half-way through the next field, still feeling stunned, and miserable, and indignant. She was so absorbed in her own sensations, that she did not hear a quick step behind her, and she was startled when Fairfax overtook her. She had no time to collect herself; she looked at him reproachfully before she knew what she was doing. He looked very ill at ease, and as if he repented the impulse which had brought him after her.

'I thought you were not going to speak to me,' she said.

'That is what I have tried to do. It is much better that I should not speak to you,' he replied; 'but I have not succeeded in carrying out my resolution, though I know that it was a wise one.'

'I don't understand,' said Bee, looking away from him because it made her heart ache so cruelly to see how haggard and ill he was looking.

'You understand that I am not a fit acquaintance for you any longer. I don't deserve that you should speak to me as your equal,' he replied, in an indifferent, matter-of-fact way.

'Mr. Fairfax, how can you say such things?' she cried. The blood rushed to her face; she looked at him with impetuous indignation in her flashing eyes. 'It is not just to me; it is not fair. You know that I always thought you a friend; you must know that I should not think of giving you up for—for this—at least if you don't know it, you must consider me a very poor creature. You ought not to assume that I am less faithful than papa has been to you.'

'You are very good and generous.'

'I am not generous at all; I am only just. Of course, if you think I can only be a fair-weather friend, you must do so. But you might be a little more generous to me. It is very wrong of you to care

46—2

so much that you hurt people's feelings to satisfy your own pride.'

A pause. Then he said in a low, reluctant tone:

' Do I hurt your feelings ?'

' Oh no, not in the least. It doesn't pain me to be told that you have resolved not to speak to me, or to know that you won't let me show you the commonest friendliness — won't even hear me say that I don't believe a word of this horrid story ! It doesn't hurt my feelings—why should it ?' she cried, in a rage with pain and mortification.

' I am sorrier than I can say if I have vexed you,' was all his answer.

He had to pray for self-control. Her face with its troubled look was so lovely, and her outspoken resentment moved him so deeply, that he had to put a strong force upon himself to keep back some frantic declaration which he durst not utter in her hearing. It was all he could do not to take advantage of her innocent friendliness, not to tell her that if she believed in him he cared for nobody else's opinion.

'But,' he went on slowly, 'it is impossible that I should continue to be your friend. In the world's opinion I am not worthy of it.'

'I have told you what I think of that.'

'You are as good as an angel to me, Miss Clare,' he said, with a thrill in his voice. 'You are a thousand times better than I deserve, for I have not had faith in your friendship. I turned out of your way just now because I was afraid that you might show me the difference that this makes between us.'

She uttered an exclamation of pained surprise: ' How *could* you ?'

' Oh, I was not afraid that you wouldn't be kind. I knew that you would be gentle and compassionate to me. You are kinder than I durst expect. You are a staunch friend. But don't you see that the more I cared for your friendship before, the harder it is for me to accept it now, when you give it on such different terms? I am grateful to you—God knows I am grateful —but——'

' Please don't. You must not talk in that way.'

' I am not so ill-conditioned as I appear; but I cannot be very gracious.'

'Oh, I know! I know! You must feel as if you hated people, and could not bear to speak to them. I am sorry that I said anything. I ought not to have troubled you—you have enough to bear. Any outsider's sympathy must be almost a mockery to you. It can do you no good.'

'Not the least. Nothing can do me any good. I am so sore that even your pity is as bad to bear as other people's scorn.'

She winced and bit her lip.

'Very well,' she said. 'I won't thrust it upon you.'

There was a silence.

'I don't pity you,' she burst out, 'in a way which could be hard to bear. How can you think I would insult you so?'

'Would you regard it as an insult to pity me?'

'Yes, certainly; in the way you mean. When you are suffering a great injustice, one wouldn't dream of pitying you as if you had fallen into trouble by your own fault.'

There was a ring of pride in her voice, and a steady light in her eyes. Such a look, such tones, were enough to give a man back his self-respect and rouse all the spirit he possessed. Yet Fairfax looked at her doubtfully.

'You do believe in me?'

'Haven't I just said so? Of course we believe in you.'

'And you don't feel as if this—injustice had marked me so that I have fallen below you? You don't shrink from my degrada-

tion and feel it an effort to treat me as you
used to do ?'

She did not answer directly; her voice
was not quite to be trusted.

'Is that what you have been feeling?' she
said at last, in a tone of grieved compassion
and pleading remonstrance.

They had reached a stile at this point,
and they stopped there. His last speech
had given Bee an insight into his state of
mind which made her feel that all attempts
to relieve his suffering were futile. As he
said himself, pity was much like scorn;
and even her tender reverent sympathy
found nothing in him which answered. As
a man who has been set in the pillory must
afterwards meet the most careless glance
with effort and shrinking, so the simplest

relations with his fellows were spoilt for Fairfax.

' That is what I have felt,' he answered drearily. ' Perhaps you can find it easier to forgive my ungraciousness when you know that.'

' It was natural that I should feel so,' he went on, as she stood mute, looking absently before her; ' you could scarcely help shrinking from a man who has fallen so low.'

' Yes, I see,' she said dreamily.

She was silent again. What could she say?

' Hadn't you better walk on ?' he said. ' Forgive me—you ought not to stand in this cold weather.'

She moved mechanically forward. He jumped over the stile, and turned to help her. She gave him her hands, and when she reached the other side, she said imploringly:

'But you know now that you were wrong?'

'Yes; I know that I was wrong about you,' he answered gently.

'I am very sorry if anything in my behaviour — I felt shy of you that last night you were at our house; but it was only because you were in trouble. And you will not imagine any more unkind things about us—that we pity you, or that this makes any difference?'

'I will only think of you as the kindest friend a man ever had,' he answered.

'Then I hope you will treat us a little more like friends for the future,' she said, smiling.

'For the future?' he echoed. 'You don't take it as a matter of course that I should go abroad and carry my misfortunes out of sight?'

'I wasn't thinking of that.'

'But when you do think of it you see that exile is my best course?'

'That must depend on how you feel yourself.'

'I should like to know what you feel.'

'It is very difficult—it isn't a question of right and wrong. Your own wishes have so much to do with it. But I don't see that it is a matter of course that you should run away. You have nothing to be ashamed of, and I wouldn't retreat before people's tongues.'

'Thank you, Miss Clare,' he replied

briefly. 'I won't run away — for the present.'

'I will turn back now,' she said, with a sudden feeling of embarrassment. 'Good-afternoon.'

She shook hands hastily—his earnest look and tone had startled her—and they parted.

The influence of her looks and words was so strongly upon Fairfax as he walked on that he scarcely missed her bodily presence. Her enthusiastic faith had sent a thrill of energy through him, and braced his courage. In the light of her earnest eyes, his cloud seemed less dark; and in the new strength which she had put into him, he felt that he might even overcome his fate—at least he could endure it with cheerfulness instead of the sullen patience he had entrenched himself in before. Her hand had pulled him out of the slough of despond, and for the first time in his life he knew what help and support a woman can give a man.

CHAPTER XXVII.

NE afternoon when dinner was over, Joe, who for some days had done nothing but sit over the fire in moody silence, opened his lips and said that he was going out. Lizzie made no opposition, though the day was cold and raw. She got his warm wraps and saw that he put them on, and begged him not to stay out long enough to catch cold.

'I'd go a little way through the

park, Joe,' she said; 'it's more sheltered there.'

But she was not surprised that Joe snarled a decided negative to this suggestion, for his temper was in a highly irritable state just then; and when that was the case, he made a point of going contrary to his wife. She wished that she had had sense enough to say nothing to him; then he might have taken the protected way instead of turning into the high-road where one felt the wind.

It was a bitter north-easter, and it blew full in Joe's face; but he walked on steadily against it, looking neither to the right hand nor to the left, till he reached Mr. Martin's house. He turned in at the garden-gate, and walked up to the house-door.

Mr. Martin was standing there, engaged

in conversation with Mr. Hammond and Mr. Young.

Joe advanced calmly to the gentlemen, who looked in some surprise at him, for he had not the manner which they were accustomed to in the poor men of the neighbourhood. Like the Yankee in 'Martin Chuzzlewit,' Joe had never 'acquired forms,' and he had no notion of touching his cap to broadcloth. He touched it occasionally—*very* occasionally—to a gentleman whom he respected personally; but he was too thorough a north-countryman not to feel himself essentially equal to any man living. He approached, therefore, with no ceremony, and said abruptly to Mr. Martin:

'Can I have a word with you, sir?'

The expression of Mr. Martin's face was

not that of lively joy or hospitable welcome.

' I can't speak to you just now,' he said.
' I'm engaged.'

' I don't wish to interrupt you,' said
Joe. ' I'll wait till you are at liberty.'

' All right,' rejoined Mr. Martin, in an
off-hand way. ' Go round to the back of
the house and rest in the kitchen till I
come. Tell them to give you some beer.'

' No, thank you,' said Joe. ' I want
no beer, and I'll not go inside. I'll wait
out here.'

He retired out of earshot, and Mr. Martin
turned to his guests, who were on horse-
back, preparing to depart.

' Isn't that the man at the Manor lodge?'
said Mr. Hammond. ' What upon earth
does he want with you?'

'I know no more than the dead. Some message, I suppose, about business. We've had dealings before.'

' You won't again, I suppose ?' said Mr. Young.

'Well, I don't see why I shouldn't,' replied Mr. Martin, in a fine spirit of liberal charity. 'Business is business, and I don't care who I do it with, provided it's at a profit,' he added.

' I'd be afraid of such a character making the profit out of me,' said Mr. Hammond, after they had laughed at the brilliant joke.

' He'd have to be pretty sharp to do *me*,' said Mr. Martin, with just self-confidence. 'I wouldn't give him a chance of coming any dodges, I can tell you.'

47—2

'I mean to have no more to do with him—business or pleasure,' said Mr. Young. Though his fears of losing by Fairfax had proved groundless, for he had received payment for the famous hay on the very day of the scene at Stonehurst, he still entertained an injured feeling that he had nearly suffered in purse. 'I like to deal with folks you can speak to.'

'Don't see why we should Boycott a poor devil in that way,' said Mr. Martin. 'He may wish to reform now, you know; and if everybody's down on him it's hard lines.'

The visitors rode off, and Mr. Martin made a reluctant step or two towards Joe, who came much more quickly towards him.

'I want to ask you a question,' he

said curtly. ' I fell in with you one night when I'd had too much, didn't I ?'

Mr. Martin nodded, and put his hands in his pockets.

' What of that ?' he demanded.

' What did I talk about then ?' said Joe, eying him sharply.

' My good fellow, what's the sense of asking me such a foolish question as that ? Do you suppose I remember the rubbish a tipsy man talks?'

' That's no answer. You can't put me off that way. I doubt I talked about Mr. Fairfax, but I can't be sure. Now, what did I say?'

' You said he was a very fine fellow,' quoth Mr. Martin lightly.

' I did talk about him, then ?' said Joe,

biting his lips. 'Look here. I mean to
know for sure. You can't fool me. Did
I tell you that he ever got into a
scrape ?'

'You talked no end of nonsense,' replied
Mr. Martin, kicking a pebble out of the
path ; and then, as Joe stood silent, he
whistled a bar of an air.

'I thought as much,' said Joe. 'I
thought it was you that spread all those
lies about him.'

'Oh, come, I say, none of that, my man,'
said Mr. Martin. 'You forget your
place.'

'My place indeed !' cried Joe furiously ;
'who are you to talk about my place ? A
sneaking cad who pumps a man when he
isn't sober, and adds a lot of big lies to
what he gets in that way, and then takes

away the character of a man that he isn't
fit to black the boots of. *My* place! Your
place ought to be a horse-pond, you
cur!'

Mr. Martin could not put down this
impertinence with the contempt he desired
to show. Any outburst of genuine passion
has a dignity and power of its own,
and Joe was so fierce in his wrath and
scorn that Mr. Martin was borne down
by his energy.

Besides, he was very uneasy in his own
breast about the part he had played in
starting the scandal. He had found it
beyond his strength to preserve silence.
The knowledge of such a startling story
was too heavy a burden for him, and
he had shared it with his neighbours, who
had surprised him by their eager acceptance

of it. He had dropped hints here and there so cautiously, that he was not credited with the beginning of the gossip, and he had a wholesome aversion to figuring as its author. He did not wish the whole part he had played to be known; he was afraid of having the anonymous letter traced to him, for that would destroy all chance of his ever winning Helen. He objected to having his action in the matter regarded in the crude way in which Joe represented it, and he winced under Joe's words. Put in that way, his deed 'stood off as gross as black from white,' and appeared a gratuitous piece of malice. Besides, he was not very clear as to what he was liable to if Fairfax should bring an action against him, and he was well aware that everybody believed and spoke a great deal more evil of him than there was any ground for asserting. So there was little dignity in his manner as he rejoined:

'That's all stuff, you know. I couldn't help your talking—you should have held your tongue. I didn't pump you; there wasn't any need. And I'll thank you to keep a civiller tongue in your head, and not use such words as "lies" to me.'

'Find me a better word. I'm not particular about being civil to *you*. What do you call the stories you've set afloat?'

'My good fellow, you're the man that sets stories afloat. How many times have you got drunk and talked at the Hare and Pheasant?'

Joe looked at him in a white rage at the taunt.

'It's no good your blackguarding *me*,' said Mr. Martin, 'because you've let the cat out of the bag. That's your own look-out; and it's a precious blue one for you, for of course your master will send you packing when he hears how you talk about him. No wonder you're put out. But, I say, look here. I've not told anyone of that prank of yours, and I shan't. You won't lose your place through me.'

'I suppose,' said Joe, eying him with grim attention, 'you call yourself a gentle-man.'

'Well, upon my soul!' ejaculated Mr. Martin, feeling outraged at this reception of his considerate assurance, which he thought must effectually soothe Joe down.

'You set up for my better,' said Joe deliberately, 'and think no small-beer of yourself; but you are the lowest cad I ever met. You'll not tell of me, won't you? Do you think that's what I came about? Do you suppose I'll keep the place, and take his wage after what I've done? You'd better tell of me; I'll tell every soul in the place, and I'll take care I'm sober when I do it. You'll see, perhaps, how much more you'll be respected for being so ready to listen to the talk of a man so much below you,' Joe laughed savagely, 'when he's tight, and then hurrying to blare it all over the shop. You should have given your authority, Mr. Martin; folks might have been less keen to listen to you then. But I'll see that they hear about it; you shall have all the credit you deserve.'

'Now, perhaps you'll take yourself off, and give me no more of your cheek,' said Mr. Martin. 'If you weren't such a poor creature, you would go away quicker than you came.'

'Lucky that I am a poor creature,' exclaimed Joe, 'if it's given me the chance to tell you what a miserable hound you are !'

And Joe turned on his heel and departed, walking firmly and quickly as long as he was on Mr. Martin's ground. But when he emerged on the high-road, he went slowly and painfully; he was not strong enough yet to bear any excitement, and he felt shattered after the scene he had just gone through.

He muttered to himself once, ' I thought that I was to be trusted.'

CHAPTER XXVIII.

A FEW days later Mrs. Somers called at Cheynehurst Vicarage. When the name was announced, Bee suppressed a slight, inhospitable unwillingness to see her visitor, and went forward with as bright a face as usual to greet her. She was very fond of the old lady, and always before to-day she had rejoiced to receive her; but now she dreaded the inevitable talk over Anthony Fairfax. Mrs. Somers would have a fresh edition of his memoirs, of course; and the effort of steeling herself to listen calmly to the calumny which was poured out over him did not become easier to Bee by repetition.

'I am sorry you did not come a little earlier, dear Mrs. Somers,' she said, when she had kissed her old friend. 'We have had luncheon; but they will bring it up directly.'

'Thank you, my dear, don't trouble,' said Mrs. Somers. 'I have had luncheon already. I have been at the Manor House.'

'At the Manor?' said Bee, rather doubtfully.

'I went to see that poor fellow whom everybody is turning his back upon. I couldn't stay away; I felt so sorry for him after all the tales I heard of the way in which people are treating him.'

' You didn't believe the stories against him ?'

'Not I. I didn't believe any one of them at first; and then my son met Mr. Clare, and heard the truth from him. It is a grievous pity. But it is no reason why his friends should give him the cold shoulder; and so I came over to show him that some folks had sense enough to stand by him.'

' It was very good of you. I am glad,' said Bee.

'I doubt whether he was glad at first sight of me,' said Mrs. Somers, laughing a little. 'He was very polite—terribly polite and formal—just as if I were a stranger and hadn't known the Fairfax

family long before he was born. But he
thawed after a while, and when he saw
I hadn't come to cross-examine him, he
was quite amiable. He is a very nice
fellow. Really, he was almost as attentive
to me as you are, my child. It was quite
pretty to see the way he laid himself out
to make me welcome.'

'Of course he would, dear Mrs. Somers,'
said Bee affectionately.

'Poor fellow! I felt so sorry for him,
alone in that dreary old house. He ought
to go away. It has told on him terribly;
he looks really ill. I should be afraid of
his breaking down if he doesn't get his
mind diverted. Your papa seems his
friend-in-chief; tell him to advise Mr.
Fairfax to leave Cheynehurst. He needs

a change. Get your papa to talk to him.'

'I will tell papa what you say.'

'I wonder he did not go at once.'

'Don't you think he might wish to show that he is not afraid of slander? If he could live it down, wouldn't it be better?'

'Ah, my dear, there is no living such a thing down, I fear; and he would have to go through more in trying to live it down than it would be worth. He has no ties to Cheynehurst—why should he trouble himself to gain the good opinion of our neighbours, who are worthy people, no doubt, but, between ourselves, are very stupid? It would be sheer waste of time for him to go on living here to be cut and slighted and insulted. If he was poor, he would have no choice. But he can leave this miserable story behind him. That will be decidedly the best thing for him.'

'Yes ; very likely,' said Bee.

'He is too sensitive to put himself in the way of being constantly reminded of what has happened. He should be helped to forget. I could see that any reference to it was like touching a raw wound. By the way,' said Mrs. Somers abruptly, 'what do you think is the last story connected with him which I heard ?'

Bee shook her head in hopeless renunciation of any attempt to guess.

'They give you as the first authority for the talk,' said Mrs. Somers, laughing.

'Me?' Bee started violently. 'Please, Mrs. Somers, tell me what you mean.'

The old lady looked in some surprise at the girl's pale, dismayed face.

'Don't disturb yourself, my dear child; you know what Cheynehurst gossip is, and nobody could believe a word of this. It is quite absurd.'

'What is it?'

'They say that you told Helen Carlyon something about Mr. Fairfax which led her to break off with him, and that that was the beginning of the talk against him. Of course it is mere chatter, and false chatter on the face of it. Why, Helen refused him months ago.'

'More than two months,' said Bee. 'Who told you this, Mrs. Somers?'

'One or two people—I forget who they were. I gave them my opinion of it, and they said they didn't believe it them-

selves; they only repeated it as a piece
of tittle-tattle. What a pity it is that
talking comes so easy to folks! If it
required a great deal of exertion, how
much we should be spared!'

'Yes, indeed,' said Bee emphatically.

'If they would even respect probability,
it would be an improvement. But they
repeat anything they hear, whether it is
likely or not. How did they come to
think of dragging you, of all people,
into it? How could you know more
about Mr. Fairfax than the rest of us?
As I told him——'

'Told whom?' said Bee quickly.

'Mr. Fairfax.'

'Did you tell *him?*'

'I mentioned it as a good specimen of
what folks can do in the way of baseless

gossip when they choose,' said Mrs. Somers carelessly. 'I did not mention Helen, of course. You need not mind, my dear; it is really a joke that they should have hit upon such an impossible story. They have dressed it up, too, with details which do great credit to their powers of imagination. One version is that you saw him in prison in his convict-dress, and only remembered him some time after he came here.'

'Oh, Mrs. Somers!' the girl said, in a choked tone.

'Ridiculous, isn't it? But gossips——'

Mrs. Somers was interrupted by the entrance of Mr. Clare. Bee moved away as the greeting was going on, and took a seat a little behind Mrs. Somers' chair.

She kept in the background while Mrs. Somers repeated what she had said already about Fairfax, and urged Mr. Clare to persuade him to go away. Mr. Clare fully agreed with her. The sooner Fairfax departed, the better for his well-being in mind and body.

'He should leave England for good,' he said emphatically.

'Tell him so.'

'Well, he isn't a person that you can press advice upon,' said Mr. Clare, showing no readiness to undertake the mission which Mrs. Somers laid upon him. 'He will go his own way.'

'Obstinate as a mule,' said Mrs. Somers elegantly. 'He looks it. But a man who has been so upset isn't fit to choose his own way; he ought to listen to his friends. It's a pity that he has nobody belonging to him to take him in hand. If he had a sister or a wife he could be made to see reason.'

'Ah, poor fellow, he isn't likely to get a wife !'

'Nonsense !' said Mrs. Somers briskly. ' He can't be condemned to lifelong single-ness because he has been unlucky. If he was unprincipled, it would be another thing; but he is a man you can trust. The very best thing for him will be to fall heartily in love with a nice girl. If he goes abroad, he can leave all this un-pleasant business behind him. The world's wide enough.'

Bee kept up a proper show of attention during Mrs. Somers' visit, but in the re-cesses of her mind she was only conscious of the fine 'specimen of gossip' which had been communicated to her. She could not dispose of it so lightly as Mrs. Somers had done; it frightened her.

Could Helen have told her aunt how she came to refuse Fairfax, and was that the way in which the gossip about him had been started? Mrs. Carlyon might have worried the reason out of Helen. If so— everything was explained.

True, there was another source from which the discovery might have come— the person who wrote the anonymous letter. But the probabilities seemed to her strongly against the theory that this stranger in the background had done the mischief. If he had written any more letters, they would have been produced by the recipients and shown to everybody ; if he had come forward and spoken, he would have been quoted. Something would have been heard of this person who knew all about Mr. Fairfax. The gossips would have been only too glad to refer to any authority who spoke with knowledge.

Besides, how could they quote Bee, unless the talk had come from the Carlyons ? There was nothing to connect her with the story if Helen remained silent. (Bee learnt later that Helen's silence had only given way under the pressure of severe cross-examination from her aunt, after the gossip of Cheynehurst reached the latter's ears.)

And having come to the conclusion that Helen must have repeated what she told her, Bee felt as bitterly regretful as if she could have helped telling her friend what she had heard. It was quite irrational, she knew ; she had had no choice in the matter ; it was not her fault that she had learnt Fairfax's secret long ago ; it would have been betrayed in any case : but yet she felt it was a cruel complication that it should be through her that it came fully to light. She had been made involuntarily— unwillingly—the instrument of hurting him ; and she felt almost as if she were to blame, and could not comfort herself by the reflection that there were other ways in which all the harm would have certainly been done.

And she was connected in people's mouths with all this hateful story. She remembered what Mrs. Somers had said about her seeing him, and it was as if a knife had pierced her heart. Somehow that association of her with him made her enter more into his pangs of shame than she had done yet; she realized them with more vivid understanding.

And he knew that people attributed the gossip about him to her. Did he give any credit to that report? What could he think of her? At the very least he must suppose that she had been chattering about his sad story, and spreading it as far as she could. No doubt he would take that view. He would not think that she meant any unkindness—only that she was a heedless chatterbox, who would entertain herself and her acquaintances with such a highly flavoured dish of gossip.

'And I professed to be his friend,'

thought Bee. 'He must hold all I said very cheap now.'

It was inexpressibly galling to think of his drawing a contrast between her words to him and her words to others. He would not be hurt; he would not care enough for such a feather-headed creature to be hurt by anything she might say or do. But he would judge of her behaviour to him differently for the future. Mrs. Somers had made it very difficult for them to be friends.

Bee imagined his strong recoil from her — his vexation at having ever treated her with any unreserve; and her dismay at the thought of his inevitable change showed her how much she prized his confidence.

It happened that Fairfax dined at the

Vicarage next day. Bee was not like herself that evening. The *insouciante* gaiety which Fairfax had thought sometimes too unclouded and careless was not visible then. But he did not like this change, and he looked at her at dinner with perplexed speculation as to its cause. She did her duty as hostess perfectly; she talked attentively to him; but her manner was subdued, and her voice had a sound of effort very unlike her usual bright tones.

After dinner Fairfax had a chance of speaking to her alone. Some one made an untimely call on Mr. Clare. In other circumstances the visitor would have been shown into the drawing-room; but, as Fairfax was there, the introduction of another person would have been awkward. Mr. Clare, therefore, went to the study.

After he had gone there was a silence in the drawing-room. Fairfax watched Bee, who was sitting in her low chair near the fire, with her hands clasped on her knee. There was a troubled look on her face, which was painfully out of character with her.

'I am afraid you are not well to-night, Miss Clare,' he said at last.

She looked at him with almost a deprecating expression in her eyes.

'Because you find me more silent than usual?'

'Well, yes, partly; and because you look out of sorts.'

'Ah, I am such a chatterbox that people expect me always to be talking,' she said, in a pained tone. 'I am quite well. But I have something to tell you, and I don't quite know how to set about it.'

'Something to tell me?' he exclaimed, in a tone of pleased expectation.

'Mrs. Somers told you something about me,' she said hesitatingly.

'Yes,' he replied indifferently. 'What of it?'

Bee opened her eyes in surprise.

'I wanted to explain—you must think me — I wanted to defend myself, in fact.'

Fairfax looked amused—purely, frankly amused.

'I didn't believe a word of it, of course. There is nothing to explain or defend. Surely you could not suspect me of thinking that you had been anything but kind.'

'Oh, I am glad! I was afraid you might think I had at least gossiped about you.'

'The idea didn't even occur to me,' he said, rather drily. 'It was more probable that people had been exercising their powers of invention. I wish they would confine them to me, and not make you their object. I felt very angry to think of their lying about you. You will not let it vex you? They mean no unkindness to you.'

'Oh, I don't care about that. But if you will let me tell you—you ought to know exactly what happened. It isn't quite false. You must forgive me for speaking of what will be disagreeable to you.'

' I am not afraid of anything disagreeable that you choose to tell me.'

Bee hastily plunged into an account of the part she had played in bringing the matter to light, making it as short as she could, and not mentioning Helen's name. She told him of the anonymous letter, and the way in which she had stumbled upon discovery of his secret. He listened with a look of perplexity, which deepened as she spoke ; but he did not say a word, and Bee's nervous dread grew. Was she destroying herself all the friendship that had been between them ?

' You ought to know,' she finished. ' You may hear false stories about the way in which it came out, and I should like you not to give me more blame than I deserve.'

'When was this?' he said.

'In January.'

'You found it out *then?*'

'Yes.'

He rose and walked away. She could make nothing of his expression; he was disturbed, but by what sort of emotions she could not discern. Was it anger which made him turn away from her?—anger which he must not express in words? But he could not find reason for anger in what she had said. But would not this knowledge of hers make him feel aversion for her, as if she had had him, unconsciously to himself, at an advantage; almost as if she had stolen into his secrets, and gained an unauthorized acquaintance with them? Bee wished heartily that she had not thought it necessary to tell him, as he walked twice or thrice the length of the room.

'You knew it, and yet you did not change to me,' he said at last, pausing near her. 'You treated me as if I was worthy to be your friend. I should like to thank you—if I knew how.'

'I remembered *all* I heard,' she said. 'They told me that it was doubted whether —and I knew you well enough to be sure that you had not deserved—that it was all a dreadful mistake.'

'You are——' he began impetuously, making a step towards her; then he stopped, and walked to the end of the room and back again. 'Is this what has been troubling you to-night?' he said, sitting down.

'Of course. I couldn't bear that you should think me such a broken reed for a friend, and I wanted you to know the exact truth. I did do you some harm—I couldn't help it, but still I am sorry for it.'

'You could not do otherwise. Don't think of it again. The whole business is not worth a sad look of yours. It was much better that the story should be known. I ought not'—he spoke with an effort—' to have kept the secret from Miss Carlyon. I had no right to keep her in the dark. But I wanted to make a fresh start, and I persuaded myself that I was justified in being silent. After all I was innocent, and it seemed unnecessary that I should be punished any more. I tried to believe that as her father had died under a cloud, that put her more on my level.'

Bee murmured an answer as he paused, an anwer which he thought was assent.

'Of course, if that had not been the case,
it would have been out of the question for
me to think of her,' he said, with a suppressed bitterness in his quiet voice. 'I was
wrong in not being open with her.'

Bee was silent.　It was very difficult to
speak of Helen, and she was wondering, with
a dart of jealous pain, what feelings his
steadily controlled tone covered.

Fairfax glanced at her quiet face, and his
brow contracted.　He went on quickly, as if
repenting that he had touched on the last
subject, and told her of the confession which
Joe Dixon had made that very afternoon.

'He is in great distress about it.　He re-
viled himself till I was obliged to defend
him.　Before I saw him Bob reproached him
unmercifully, I understand, and the poor
fellow is quite broken down.　He intends to

punish himself by leaving the lodge at once, and I could not persuade him to change his mind. I hope he will, for he is scarcely fit to go back to work yet.'

'It is very kind of you to wish him to stay after this,' said Bee.

'No,' replied Fairfax gravely, 'it is not kindness. It is merely the payment of a debt. I will tell you about it—some time.'

Bee was glad that the explanation was made, and that it had not been required. But Fairfax looked back on the evening with profound dissatisfaction. Their talk, while it relieved her, had only depressed him.

The terms on which they associated were intolerable. At first she had done him good. But this effect did not last, and he was beginning to find that her society only cast him down further. It drove further and further home the realization of 'all his own mischance.' He lifted hopeless eyes to her, and the hopelessness tormented him.

He felt ungratefully that her friendship and gentleness were of no profit to him ; it was all cold compared with what he would fain have won from her. It must be something closer than sympathy, more tender than kindness, to content him.

He remembered with a sore chafing how, when he had learnt that her faith in him had been so thorough that it had not waited even for his assurance that he was innocent, he had longed to tell her that he loved her, and he had felt it impossible. At her words a flood of passionate emotion had swept over him as if it must find a way, and yet he had been constrained to silence. He was not proud of his self-command ; he was bitterly resentful of the circumstances which put them so far apart that he must only be her friend.

She herself had unwittingly galled him terribly by her manner. It was so calm and frankly kind. She was quite at her ease with him, and not at all afraid of listening to his confidences : she did not imagine that there was any danger of his drifting into anything so mad as love for herself; she felt safe from any attempt on his part to approach her as a lover. Did his degradation make such a difference between them that she thought it out of the question for him to forget himself so far?

Of course. Had she not agreed with him that only a girl whose position resembled his own could fairly be thought of as his wife ?

CHAPTER XXIX.

'We are not peers
So to be lovers ; and I own, and grieve,
That givers of such gifts as mine are, must
Be counted with the ungenerous.'

MRS. BROWNING.

EXT day Bee went to pay a visit to the lodge. She had not been there for some time. She had kept away since Fairfax's story had come out, feeling a reluctance to see his servants while he was being so unmercifully talked of, and dreading to hear them speak of it.

It was a dull day in March, cold as

January, and with heavy rain-clouds drifting over a leaden sky. A short distance
from the park gates a shower began to fall,
and Bee's cloak was wet by the time she
reached the lodge. Lizzie met her at the
door, relieved her of her cloak, and expressed
a subdued pleasure at seeing her. She
looked worried and anxious, and sighed
when Bee asked after her husband.

'He's only poorly, ma'am, thank you.
Will you walk in ? There's a fire in here,'
opening the door into the little parlour. 'I
lit it for Joe, because I'm washing to-day,
but he hasn't come downstairs at all. He'll
be sorry to miss seeing you.'

'Shall I be in your way, Mrs. Dixon ?
Are you too busy to talk to me ?'

'Oh no, Miss Clare. I'm glad you've
come. The work can wait a bit, and Joe

doesn't want me just now. Mr. Fairfax has
gone up to speak to him. Sit down here
and dry your feet, or you'll be taking
cold.'

They had talked for a little while, when a
step was heard on the stairs. Lizzie started
up, and went out.

'Won't you wait till it fairs, sir?' Bee
heard her say. 'Come into the front room.
Miss Clare is here.'

'No, thank you. I am afraid I must be
going,' said Fairfax's voice. 'Good-afternoon,' and the door was opened.

'But the rain, sir! It's quite a down-
pour; you'll get wet through going up to
the Manor House. It's coming down in
washing-tubsful. Do wait a bit!'

'Well, it is rather heavy. Perhaps I
had better wait.'

Bee heard the door shut, and he came in, and shook hands. Lizzie put some coal on, said that Joe would be wanting her, and went upstairs. Joe did not receive her with much amenity. He observed that she'd better go and talk to Miss Clare; it wasn't manners to leave her.

'Mr. Fairfax is there, and they can talk to each other,' said Lizzie. 'They'll like that better than talking to me.'

A brilliant idea had started into her head, and she felt sure that the most acceptable thing she could do was to efface herself, and leave her guests to themselves.

Fairfax, after a greeting which to his own consciousness was stiff and awkward, went to the window, and looked attentively at the rain, which quite justified Lizzie's description. He made some remarks about the weather, to which Bee, who did not see in his manner what he felt was there, replied in her usual way. Every commonplace self-possessed speech vexed him, and made him feel more constrained. He wanted to avoid her presence, with its mocking suggestions, and she did not even perceive that he was ill at ease with her.

' Yes, you had better wait till this shower is over,' she was saying coolly. ' It is too violent to last.'

Her composure helped him to control himself. He shook off quickly the imbecile weakness which had rushed over him on hearing she was in the house. There was no danger of his betraying himself. Why should he? He had loved her long enough, and he had kept silence; he would not now risk offending her by any ridiculous confession.

'The rain will be over in ten minutes,' he said, turning round. 'Shall I fill up the time by telling you how I came to know the Dixons?'

'If you will, I should like to hear.'

'I want to tell you also my version of my story. I have wished and intended for some time to be quite open about it, and this is a good opportunity.'

He chose that time with a certain perverse instinct of self-torment. It would serve to tame the longings which had leapt to such strength lately to go over the history which in every sentence must make him feel the folly of desiring her love. It would be a safeguard against his own

daring fancies to make his position as clear
to her eyes as it ought to be to his
own.

‘It happened more than five years ago,
when I was twenty-three years old. I was
a clerk in the business of a relation of my
father's—I called him my uncle, but he really
was a second cousin. My father and mother
both died when I was a boy at school, and
my relations brought me up among them.
When I was old enough, this cousin gave
me employment. I was rather a trial to
him. I did not like my work ; it was
horribly monotonous, and it was dispiriting
to look forward to being a clerk all my
days. It didn't seem possible to get up
any enthusiasm for an occupation which
held out such a limited prospect. My
uncle was enraged at my idleness, and

horrified at some discontented grumblings of mine which came to his ears. I got a bad character with him. I did some foolish things; I never did anything worse than foolish, but my doings were exaggerated to my uncle till he regarded me as a reprobate. I got into a little debt, which he heard of; and I was stupid enough to lose some money at cards and billiards.

'One night when I was at my uncle's house, he asked me to pay the account of a tradesman for him; and, instead of a cheque, he gave me the money in bank-notes, which he happened to have in the house. I went to do it at once, but when I got to the man's shop, it was shut. On my way back, I fell in with my uncle's only son. My cousin Walter was about my own age. His father believed him to be a pattern of all that a young man ought to be, but in reality he was very extravagant. He contrived to take his amusements so cautiously that very few people knew he indulged in them, and he was regarded in the town with great respect. He had always been kind to me, and I liked him ; he took my part with his father when I got into trouble at the office, and he seemed my friend.

'I told him where I had been, and said it was provoking to have missed the man, as I was going away next day for a short holiday, and I didn't want to put off my start in the morning. He said he would pay the man for me. I handed the notes over to him, and——' Fairfax stopped for a moment, and added in a bitter tone, 'thanked him.'

'You can guess what happened. My worthy cousin kept the money for himself. He needed money badly at the time, and this came too opportunely. It was a large sum, and the temptation must have been great. I don't believe he wished to do me any harm ; but he felt obliged to save himself, and I was not so important a person as he was. No doubt he supposed that it was safe enough, and that he would not be found out. My uncle was going away for a long absence, and as Walter was to have charge of the business, he could make things straight. Unluckily my uncle fell ill, and was longer in leaving home than he had intended ; and just before he was starting, he met this tradesman, and heard he had not been paid.

'He sent for me at once. I told him my

story, which my cousin contradicted point-
blank in every particular. He had never
received any money from me ; he had never
undertaken to pay this bill ; he knew
nothing about it. I was making a strange
mistake. He was quite cool and moderate ;
he soothed my uncle when he accused me
of lying, and was horrified when he talked
of theft. That was impossible. I must
have been robbed myself, or I might have
lost the money. But he inclined to the
view that I had been robbed when I—I was
intoxicated, in fact,' said Fairfax, flushing.
' So he cleverly insinuated a fresh charge,
that I was in the habit of drinking, which
was as well deserved as the other.

' My uncle was, as he thought, very
lenient to me. He told me that he could
excuse me if I had lost the money, either

by my own carelessness, or robbery, as my cousin suggested. If I would confess and withdraw my shameful attempt to throw the blame on Walter, he would hush the matter up. But I was obstinate, and refused to retract a word I had said. I am not sure now whether I was foolish or not. Perhaps it would have been wiser to submit to blame for carelessness, and let the thing blow over; but I was too angry with my cousin to calculate consequences, and I knew very well how galling it would be to be treated in the future as a person who was not to be trusted.'

He paused. Up to that point he had spoken quietly and steadily; now he seemed to have a difficulty in going on.

'Don't tell me any more,' said Bee. 'I
see how it happened.'

'I must tell you. Some of the notes
were traced to a man in the town, who
swore I had given them to him in payment of a bet. I was tried, and of course
I hadn't a chance. The very lawyer who
defended me showed me that he did not
believe my account, and he advised me
to set up another defence, as that would
only do me harm. But I was not afraid.
I could not believe but that somehow I
should be cleared. I was astounded when
this man gave his evidence, and coolly
swore my character away; I was thunder-
struck when the verdict was given, and
the sentence passed.'

'Don't—oh, don't!' she said.

'The day I saw you first, when you

offered me those flowers, was the day of my release. I can't tell you how I felt after that awful year—I don't like to think of it.'

He went on to tell her about his illness, and the kindness he had received in it. His account was very brief and simple, and perhaps by those qualities it touched her the more. He did full justice to the Dixons' hospitality, and spoke of his debt to them with an absence of false shame which Bee thought admirable. Then he talked of his life since; of the dreariness he had endured, and the loneliness which grew hateful; and of the good which the friendship of the Clares had done him.

Bee listened, with now and then a word which drew him on to say more: she understood how great the relief must be to talk of it, but she asked no questions.

What he told her should be entirely of his own choice and will.

Every now and then, through the pain which the tale gave her, a thrill of joy and pride made itself felt, because he chose her to listen to it, because he looked for her sympathy, and trusted in it.

'I never talked about it to anyone before,' he said at last.

'I am glad you have talked about it now,' rejoined Bee quickly; then, afraid of betraying her own intense interest, she added: 'It will do you good to speak of it.'

'Thank you, yes,' he said, rather coldly. 'You are very kind to listen to me, Miss Clare. I had no idea that I was expatiating at such length. Forgive me for the infliction.'

'Oh, but I liked it,' she said, seeing that he was drawing back into his shell, and remorseful for giving him the notion that it was for his benefit that she had turned an attentive ear. 'I liked it very much—that is, of course I am very sorry——' she broke off, blushing and embarrassed. 'You understand what I mean. I am very sorry you have such sad things to tell, but I am glad that you told me.'

She was looking up at him—her eagerness to explain away the unpleasant impression he had received from her former reserved speech shining in her eyes, but he did not meet her gaze.

'You are very kind,' he said in formal, measured tones. 'I ought not to have told you,' he said, after a pause. 'It isn't a fit tale for your ears. You cannot put any interest into it; it is only vulgar, hateful, and degrading. I fancied that I could bear your knowing it, but I have made an egregious blunder.'

'If it has given you pain——' she began. He interrupted her.

'Pain? You don't understand. It is monstrous that a man should have to tell such a tale to you.'

'But I do not mind,' she said, only thinking of showing him that she did not shrink from his painful history, that what he called vulgar and degrading did not disgust her.

'I know you will endure the unpleasantness of it for the sake of kindliness,' he answered, speaking irritably, as a man might speak who is in severe physical pain. 'You need not mind. It is far enough from you. I would not have told you if I had thought it would grieve or shock you too much. I felt that I owed it to you and Mr. Clare to be frank with you, and I fancied that it would be easier to tell you. But I did not know how hideous it was till I had told you. I thought I was ashamed of it before—I thought I hated it enough before; but you make it blacker. Oh my God !' he cried, almost under his breath, 'that I should have to tell *you* such horrors—*you*——'

There was a dead silence, in which Bee was only conscious that her heart was beating wildly, chokingly, and that he was standing away from her with averted face. She could neither move nor utter a word: she could only breathlessly wait for him to look at her, to speak to her.

'You whom I love,' he went on firmly and rapidly ; 'you whom, if this hateful thing did not stand between us, I should beg to give me your love, instead of pity and kindness. I have no right to tell you—I thought I should never dare to tell you that I love you ; but it is out now. It was too much to think of the contrast between what my life has been made and what I might have hoped for if I had been like other men. I might have tried to win you. Now I must not even dream of it. Oh, my love, to lose that chance is the bitterest loss of all !'

A faint, inarticulate murmur came from her lips, and she made a movement with her hands as if to stop him.

'You are displeased with me, of course, and I deserve your displeasure. I am presuming unwarrantably on your goodness to

me. Forgive me. I will not trouble you
any longer.'

'Oh, hush!' she cried. 'You must not
talk so.'

'I know it,' he said, in a perfectly self-
possessed tone. He had mastered his agitation. 'It can only offend and annoy you.
I will go now.' He made a step or two
towards her, hesitatingly. 'Will you say
good-bye to me?' then, as she did not put
out her hand: 'Have I offended you so
deeply?'

'No ; I am not offended,' she faltered.
She held out her hand mechanically, but she
did not look up. 'I—I——' her voice broke
in a sob.

'You are sorry for me!' he exclaimed,
half tenderly, half angrily. 'I don't need
your pity for *this.*'

He took her hand and showered passionate kisses on it.

'Good-bye,' he said, at last. He still held her hand, as if he could not bear to let it go of his own will ; but the close pressure was relaxed, and she could have drawn it away and dismissed him at once. She did not move. Her hand lay passively in his.

' Say that you forgive me all the trouble I have given you. Let me have one more kind word to go away with.'

She looked up at him. She was very pale, and the muscles about her lips were set as if with some resolution. Their eyes met for a second, then her head drooped, and hot colour rose in to her cheeks.

' Don't go,' she said, with a great effort.

A bewilderment of joy and incredulity came over his face, and for an instant he

stood motionless ; then he seemed to wake
up to full comprehension of what she had
confessed, and to see that she was hiding
her face from him. He knelt down beside
her ; he forgot, in the rush of surprise, everything but the exultant tenderness which a
man must feel when he first learns that his
love is accepted and returned.

'My darling,' he said unsteadily, ' do you
care what I do ? Can you really care a
little for me ?'

' I do.'

' Won't you lift up your head and look at
me ?'

She dropped her hands; he drew her to
him, all his passionate worship in the gaze
he bent upon her, and kissed her. But
directly after, a heavy cloud darkened his
face.

'I ought not to love you ; it can only bring you misfortune.'

' I am not afraid.'

' Not after all that has happened to me ?'

' Not a bit.'

' My love, my poor little love!' he said, still with that dark look of gloom.

' If I am your love I don't consider myself poor,' she said, with a shy pride in her earnest eyes.

' If you are !'   And he poured out an ardent avowal of all she had been to him, all she was.   He told her how at the very first he had been drawn towards her, and his evil fate crossed the way and made him feel that she was not for him ; how her very brightness had driven him away, because it was so unlike his own sadness ; how his feeling for her had been spoilt, and he had fancied that some one else would be a fitter mate for him, yet he had never fully shaken off her power.

'And when you stood by me and believed in me, how could I help forgetting all that made it madness for me to love you ? How could I help worshipping you, though I was unworthy to kiss the hem of your dress ? You may be very sure that I love you. I have not known whether it has been my greatest misfortune or my greatest blessing, but you have taken all my heart.'

'It must be a blessing now,' she whispered.

He kissed her again, but he made no answer in words ; and after a brief pause she started up.

'I must be going. Isn't the rain less heavy now ? Yes, it is nearly over.'

They went out into the gloomy afternoon.
Bee did not notice the raw, damp air, nor
the chilly sky overhead, nor the thick mud
beneath her feet. She was in a world which
knew nothing of small, outward discomforts.
Her heart was full of the strange, solemn
satisfaction which attends on all deep
emotion ; she was engrossed with the bliss
of knowing that Fairfax loved her. Her
happiness was grave and quiet, and she was
quite content that the walk home should be
taken in almost unbroken silence.

'I cannot come in,' said Fairfax, when
they came to the garden-gate. 'I will come
to-morrow.'

'Very well. Good-bye till to-morrow,
then.'

'Till to-morrow,' he repeated. 'Good-
bye, my darling—God bless you !'

As she went up the path she turned back to smile a last greeting, and wave her hand; and he carried away in his mind a picture of her face, pale and a little wistful, with a great tenderness shining in her eyes, smiling at him out of the grey mist. It was a picture which should have aroused contented and joyful reflections ; but he grew sadder as he dwelt on it.

His joy had been very brief, and a hopeless gloom settled down on him now. He could only bring her sorrow : he was so sure of that, that out of her presence he could not see a ray of hope. Even the knowledge of her love made his burden of melancholy foreboding heavier by adding self-reproach to it.

What right had he to take such gifts from her ? They did not do him good, and they left her robbed of her serenity and glad enjoyment of life. For her love he could give her only disappointment and regret.

CHAPTER XXX.

'I will not soil thy purple with my dust,
    Nor breathe my poison on thy Venice-glass,
Nor give thee any love—which were unjust.
    Beloved, I only love thee! let it pass.'
                                MRS. BROWNING.

BEE said nothing to prepare her father for the interview which she supposed Fairfax intended to seek to-morrow. The reason for her silence was perhaps rather peculiar. Under other circumstances, she would have told her father what had happened, and sought from him some of the sympathy which happier girls can ask from a mother. But she knew that there were difficulties before her and Fairfax. Her exceeding happiness did not blind her to them. Her father would not like the engagement, and he would express himself to that effect to Fairfax, who would have trouble in removing his objections. She did not expect positive refusal of consent—only disagreeable surprise, hesitation, and coldness—opposition, which they must overcome by patience. They would have to wait for consent; submit to some probation; perhaps be separated for a time, till Mr. Clare was assured that they were both in earnest. She did not expect smoothness and pleasantness at all. But her father would not push his natural unwillingness to give his daughter to such a suitor beyond a certain limit, and when he found that she was firmly attached to Fairfax he would give in.

It was very sorrowfully that she contemplated any clashing with her father's will. It was the first time in her life that she had seriously thought of opposing him, and it was sad that she must do it for Fairfax's sake. But since it was for Fairfax's sake, she must bear whatever came.

As she anticipated difficulty, she made no attempt to smooth the way for Fairfax by starting the subject with her father. The two men must deal with each other: she must not come between to ward off any disagreeables from her lover. It would not be to his dignity if she tried to coax her father into giving a more favourable hearing ; Fairfax must speak for himself.

Her fears of the way in which Mr. Clare would take it, her confident looking forward to a period of waiting, did not damp her joy. It was too deep to be easily affected. She was too blessed in knowing that their hearts had met to indulge in serious forebodings. Everything must turn out well in time; and they were young, and had love and confidence to make them patient and strong.

It was about eleven o'clock next morning when she heard Fairfax's ring at the door. She was in the schoolroom, giving the boys their lessons, and so far she had paid as much attention as usual to them ; but after that sound she could not fix her mind on the mysteries of vulgar fractions, in which Eustace was darkly and querulously groping.

'That will do for the present,' she said, laying down the slate-pencil. 'You may put your books away, boys.'

The boys obeyed at once, and hurried out: 'theirs not to make reply,' when such an agreeable irregularity as dismissal an hour too soon was in question. Bee went to the morning-room, and prepared herself to wait; but a quarter of an hour had scarcely passed, when she heard the study-door open, and steps cross the hall. Her father looked in.

'Ah, I thought you would be here, Bee,' he said, in a quiet, non-committal tone. He withdrew, and next minute Fairfax appeared.

He was very pale, with a fagged look
and dull eyes, as though he had not slept
during the night. He paused for a
moment, as if doubtful how to address her;
then:

' I have come to say good-bye to you,'
he said abruptly.

' Must you go away?' she said, a little
tremor in her voice.

' Yes.'

' But you will come back?'

' How can I?'

She looked at him with mute inquiry.
There was a piteous dismay and bewilderment in her face—she was startled by
his abrupt manner—and her hands were
trembling.

He saw the quivering fingers, and caught
them in his. The cold, fixed expression

left his face ; there was passionate love and trouble in it.

' My darling—oh, my darling !' he cried remorsefully, kissing the cold, passive hands.

' You are going to leave me—for good ?' she said incredulously.

He bent his head. He was still holding her hands, and he felt her start of pain and the shudder which ran through her. He drew her to the couch, and sat down beside her.

' Why ?' she said distinctly.

He made an impatient movement.

' You know that I must go. I cannot stay near you after yesterday. I must not ask you to be my wife, and there is nothing for it but for me to take myself out of your sight. I have acted like a weak, dishonourable fool in letting you see how I care for you, and in taking advantage of your divine pity.'

Bee had expected to hear that it was on account of her father's objections that he was banishing himself, and she was ready to undergo separation till Mr. Clare should consent. But Fairfax said nothing of her father. He spoke of his own resolution as if it depended on no one else.

'Has papa refused?'

'It is not that which makes me see the wrong I have done you. I give you up because I cannot do otherwise. He would refuse if I were mad enough to ask him to give you to me. You must forget me as quickly as you can; that will be the best thing for you.'

'Do you advise me to do that?' she

asked, with a faint shade of derision in her voice.

He looked at her earnestly, and said gravely, almost solemnly:

'Yes. I would rather be forgotten by you than know that I have given you sorrow. And I can only be a cause of pain to you.'

'Do you really care for me?' she said irrelevantly.

'Need you ask?'

'Tell me again,' she said softly, while hot colour rose to her forehead, 'do you care for me so much that you would—— if there was nothing in the way—do you care for me more than anybody else, or is it a fancy because you are lonely and I have shown you sympathy?'

'I love you better——' he began, and

broke off, half laughing. ' There is no comparison possible. I love you with all my heart. There is nobody in the world but you for me—nobody. Whatever happens, you must believe that.'

' Then why must you give me up ?' she said, in a whisper.

He took her close to his heart, and for a little while there was silence. He had no words to say; he could only hold her tight in his arms, with an impotent defiance of the circumstances which cut her off from him. It was easy comparatively to give her up in his own mind, at the bidding of his own conscience and honour; but when she pleaded with him against that decree, it seemed far beyond his strength to renounce her. He kissed the soft hair as she hid her face on his shoulder, and one or two hot tears fell on the bright masses.

' You are doing it out of regard for me,' she said, in a quick, low tone. 'I know how you feel. You are very proud, and you think it would be wrong to be engaged to me while you are under a cloud. But I don't see it so. And if I am not afraid of your trouble, why should we not bear it together?'

' You are brave enough, my dearest. But how can I let you sacrifice yourself to me? I cannot—I dare not.'

' Sacrifice!' she said, a little impatiently. 'What has that to do with it? You forget that—I care for you. It would be a sacrifice to try to forget you, as you talk of my doing; but to help you to be happy—I thought I could,' in a wistful tone which was very pathetic—' that wouldn't be a sacrifice.'

' Don't,' he said sharply. ' You wring my heart. I cannot bear it.'

He moved away from her, shading his face with his hand. She looked a little perplexed, then an eager, hopeful look broke over her face, and she leant forward and laid her hand on his sleeve.

' Don't you see ?' she urged. ' Don't you understand my side of it ?'

He did not turn towards her, and he did not make any answer.

' Listen to me,' the sweet voice went on. ' You say you love me; doesn't that give me a right to speak ? You are wrong in your way of looking at this— quite wrong. You give me up because you have got a morbid impression about yourself: you make yourself more un-happy than ever. Well, I suppose you have a right to choose to be unhappy, if you will; but you haven't quite so certain a right to make me unhappy. Oh, I know what you think!' as he was about to speak; 'you think this way will make me less unhappy than the other. But,' and her voice dropped, 'you are mistaken.'

'Yes; it has come to this, that one way or another you must be unhappy through me,' he said gloomily; 'but at least I can choose the unhappiness which I shall not profit by. I have been selfish towards you, and it is too late to undo the harm which I have done. You are the most generous woman in the world;

but I cannot let your life be spoilt by
me. I could never forgive myself for
bringing my blight upon you. It is bad
enough to know that my name is what
it is ; but if it was yours—— Besides,'
he added more calmly, ' there is another
consideration. You forget that your father
would never consent. He could not give
his child to a disgraced man. You are
meant for something better than that.
You could not disobey him, you know.'

'No, of course I would not. But—if
we waited—he might consent.'

Fairfax only shook his head.

' We could wait till you are cleared,' she
suggested.

He smiled—a faint, bitter smile.

' My dearest, it would be wicked to
waste your youth in that way. No;

there is only one thing for me to do, to leave you quite free, and give up all claim to you.'

Bee sat pale, mute, and rigid. She was not convinced, but she could not say another word. Perhaps some slight touch of the mortification of a woman who has offered more than a man will accept, made itself felt by her. She would have clung to him with unflinching faithfulness, if he had willed it so. But as he renounced her without any struggle to win her, she could only submit to his decision.

She understood why he acted so, and recognised in a far-off way that it might seem to him an imperative duty to give her up—a duty exacted by honour and love for her. But she could only feel that he was cruel in leaving her. She could not acquiesce in the necessity which inflicted this benumbing misery upon her.

'I wish you would reproach me,' he said almost violently, as he looked at her white, set face. 'How dare I drag you into my troubles ?'

'What is there to reproach you for ?'

'It is part of my curse that you must suffer through me. It is only wretchedness for you to care for me. I must be sorry that you do—instead of being proud and glad.'

'Oh, hush! Don't be sorry. I should like you to be proud of it,' she said, with an attempt at smiling. . 'You must not speak so hopelessly. Have you really no hope that things will come right ?'

'None.'

'Oh, Anthony!' she said pitifully, her

faint resentment of his renunciation swept away in tenderness for his evident suffering. She forgot the pride which would have made her stand on her dignity with him at any other time; she could not think of herself just then. 'I shall hope. This cannot be the end—I *cannot* believe it is. You will be cleared some day.'

'God grant your hopes may be fulfilled!' he said fervently. 'Perhaps they may be, as they are yours.'

'Yes, you must put faith in them, and believe that they will come true. I shall not be wretched—I shall only wait——'

'Oh, my poor darling!' he broke in, 'you must not say such things to me. You must not promise me anything, and I must not promise you anything, except that I will never trouble you again. That

is what I have told your father—that I
will keep away from you. This *is* the end
for me. Do you suppose I would give
you up if there was the least chance
that I could ever offer you an unstained
name ? Don't I know that you would
wait ? I know very well what I am
giving up—how true and good you are,
and how happy it would make me to
know that you thought of me, even if I
did not see you. But I should be even
meaner than I have shown myself towards
you already if I let you bind yourself in
any way. A sharp wrench now will be
easier for you than to grow sick at heart
waiting for years and years. I am not
worth it, dearest.'

'Don't say such things about yourself,'
she said faintly. 'They hurt me.'

There was a long pause, filled for each with the bitterness of hopeless loss and imminent parting.

'I must go,' said Fairfax at last.

'Are you going to leave Cheynehurst at once?' she asked mechanically.

'Yes. I must not see you again. I cannot stay here.'

'No. Good-bye then,' she said abruptly, hastening to say the words she dreaded, as men sooner than bear fear will rush on a danger which they shrink from in their hearts.

They looked at each other, and something in his eyes made her hold out her hands with a despairing, passionate cry.

'Oh, my poor Anthony, must you go? I love you so, and it does you no good.'

She was strained close in his arms, and she clung to him with no more thought of reserve than if he had been dying.

He gave her a long passionate kiss of farewell, but he did not speak; and when she dashed away the tears which had blinded her eyes, she was alone.

CHAPTER XXXI.

AIRFAX went away at once. He rapidly made arrangements that the work which he had undertaken in the neighbourhood should be carried on without him; he forgot nothing that depended on him. Mr. Hurst, his man of business, was much impressed by the thoroughness with which he put his affairs in order, and the care with which he remembered every point that must be settled; and meeting Mr. Clare and his daughter one day in the village, he spoke warmly of his employer's business faculty.

'He has a very good head,' he said approvingly. 'He had thought of everything, and he gave me as full directions as if he were settling things for the last time. I'm afraid it'll be long before we see him back again. He seemed to wish to have all his affairs settled. He made his will when he was in London.'

'Ah!' said Mr. Clare vaguely.

'I had to go up and see him before he left finally, and I heard that it had been made. I wonder who he's left his money to. I'm to pay so much over to you, Mr. Clare, every year, for you to use for the poor as you think fit; but of course he told you that. He gave me a list of people that he specially wished to be looked after, and I have to send it to you. He said you would excuse his not giving it to you himself, as he was called away so suddenly.'

'Oh yes, of course,' said Mr. Clare. 'Let me have it. I will do what he wishes. Good-morning,' he added, cutting the talk short with less than his usual urbanity.

Mr. Hurst, who was prepared to gossip at some length about Fairfax, and had hoped by judicious questioning to find out if Mr. Clare was acquainted with the reason of his sudden departure, felt slightly aggrieved by this abruptness; and consoled himself by the mental utterance of a cynical generalization as to people's faithfulness to unlucky friends.

Mr. Clare had not dared to look at Bee while Mr. Hurst talked. He was in positive pain for what he imagined she was feeling; and he would have liked to express some of his sympathy in a delicate and indirect way if he had known how. But he hated the subject too much to feel it anything but difficult to approach it. He had never referred to it, except to utter a few commonplace speeches on the day when Fairfax had bade her good-bye; and he was afraid that if he suggested consolations now she might break down and shed tears. He had not seen any tears yet, but the fear of them was strong upon him. So he preserved an awkward silence, waiting till she might be presumed to have recovered from the agitation which hearing of Fairfax must cause, and it would not be against the etiquette of sentiment to talk of indifferent things. He was surprised when she spoke.

' Papa, you will look well after the people for him ?'

Her tone was quite calm, and there was no trace of emotion in her expression.

' Yes, yes ; certainly, my dear.'

' Will you let me see his list ? Perhaps I could do something—if you will let me.'

' Yes, you shall do as you like. The people must not suffer through his absence. It was very good of him to attend so care-fully to them,' said Mr. Clare, bestowing this mild encomium with a certain grudge.

' It was like him,' said Bee proudly.

' Poor fellow !' escaped Mr. Clare's lips.

' Please, papa,' she said, smiling up at him, ' don't call him that. I don't like the phrase at all, and it doesn't suit him.'

Mr. Clare was silent. He would have willingly undertaken never to call Fairfax anything again ; he wished fervently not to speak of him nor to hear him spoken of. He was full of anger with him for daring to raise his eyes to his darling child. Any man who had made love to Bee would have been regarded by Mr. Clare with strong disfavour, and would have needed many merits to escape condemnation as a presuming and conceited person. But that Fairfax, with his disadvantages, should love her and tell her so, was not to be borne.

When Mr. Clare learnt that he had been ill-advised enough to betray his feelings, he felt with disgust that it was quite a mistake to show friendship to a young man under a cloud. Such a heroic undertaking was not for a man who had a marriageable daughter.

He was spared the unpleasantness of expressing his sense of Fairfax's conduct by the latter's vehement self-blame. He had been weak, selfish, mad, presumptuous. Mr. Clare had only to assent by silence. He was thankful that Fairfax had right feeling enough not to make any attempt to entangle Beatrice in an endless, hopeless engagement; and he would have been sorry for him if he could have forgiven him for the fact that Bee returned his affection. But there was no forgiveness for that in Mr. Clare's heart. It was atrocious to win her liking under the circumstances; and he felt this all the more bitterly, because he blamed himself for allowing the girl to see so much of Fairfax.

' Her mother would have been wiser,' he thought sadly.

He could only hope that Bee had not
been much injured by his carelessness, and
that she would get over the unfortunate
affair quickly. She would surely forget
when there was nothing to stir up any
romantic notions of faithfulness to Fairfax·
He had renounced her completely; and he
had, without being asked, given Mr. Clare
his word that he would never return to the
neighbourhood again, nor attempt to com-
municate with her. Bee would be sad for a
little while; but her youth and her elastic
temperament would enable her to throw off
her disappointment.

He was encouraged in this hope by the
way in which from the very first she behaved. She turned as cheerful a face as
ever to the world, and went through her
daily routine as steadily and diligently as

before. There was no outward mourning. Mr. Clare soon ceased to feel for her, and to dread an inopportune burst of emotion when chance references to Fairfax were made in conversation, for she always bore them with equanimity. There could not be much amiss with her, her father decided, as he watched her anxiously, and detected no signs that she was drooping; her heart had only been lightly touched.

She was forgetting him, Mr. Clare thought, as time passed and she went about as usual, unchanged in manner, gay and bright, taking apparently as much interest as ever in all she did, as loving to him and her brothers.

Never had an unfortunate love affair been so easily disposed of. Mr. Clare's admiration for his daughter grew as he found he

was to escape any discomfort from her indulgence in sentimental regrets and wilful
pining.   She was behaving with great sense
and spirit.

PART III.

CHAPTER I.

IT was August, more than a year since the day when Fairfax had said good-bye to Beatrice. She was at the seaside with the boys, who had just gone through the measles, and old Mrs. Somers had joined the party. Mr. Clare was spending his holiday in a trip to Switzerland.

One afternoon Bee was sitting in the window of Mrs. Somers' sitting-room, waiting to go out with her friend for the saunter which it was her ' custom always of the afternoon ' to take at the seaside. The old lady had just finished a nap, and was drinking an early cup of tea to restore her forces. and as she sipped she glanced now and again at Bee.

Mrs. Somers had no suspicion of the affair with Fairfax, and certainly there was nothing in Bee's face to betray that the past sixteen months had not been cloudless. There were no lines of discontent about her mouth : there was no shadow on her brow. Mrs. Somers smiled with involuntary pleasure in the sweetness of the looks of the girl who held to her something of the place of a petted granddaughter, as she gazed at the fair face, fresh as the morning.

Turning round from a long contemplation of the sea, Bee met Mrs. Somers' eyes.

' A penny for your thoughts,' said the old lady.

' It would not be so easy to say what they were,' said Bee, laughing. ' Thoughts get so tangled sometimes that one cannot straighten them out presentably. I was dreaming a little, and looking at the water. What were you thinking about, Mrs. Somers ?'

' Well, my dear, though you don't deserve a more satisfactory answer than you have given me, you shall have one. I was thinking about you.'

' I hope you weren't thinking that my dress is too plain for the promenade this afternoon ?'

' Of course not. Your dress is very pretty,' said Mrs. Somers, with an abstracted glance at the fresh white cambric. ' I was wishing that I could persuade you to take a bit of advice.'

'What is the advice ?'

'Well, it is about Mr. West.'

'Ah,' said Bee, in an uninterested tone.

'You tiresome child, you put an end to my discourse before I have begun. That dry monosyllable says that my wisdom will be thrown away on you.'

Bee smiled a little in a teasing fashion.

'I want you to think about him with a little interest. You must have discovered that he admires you.'

'Yes,' said Bee frankly. 'I know he does, and I am sorry for it.'

'I should be very glad if you could like him in return.'

'Oh, I cannot,' said Bee energetically. 'There is no chance of my doing that.'

'You are very sure about it,' said Mrs. Somers, smiling. 'You need not decide against him so firmly. You might give him a chance of winning your good graces. What objection can you have to him ?'

'None personally. But, dear Mrs. Somers, pray believe that I shall never care more for him than I do now,'said Bec, with unwonted gravity. 'Indeed, indeed I cannot. It is quite out of the question. Please don't talk of it any more.'

'My dear child, don't disturb yourself so much about it. You take it too seriously.'

The girl's agitation was quite out of proportion to the occasion. She was pale, and there was a shrinking look in her eyes as if she was being urged to do something distasteful or wrong. She recovered herself as Mrs. Somers looked wonderingly at her.

' I won't take it seriously if you will not
be Mr. West's advocate,' she said, smiling,
' and if you will promise not to encourage
him. I do what I can to show him how I
feel. It really is not my fault that he thinks
of me,' she said, in a deprecating tone.

' No, indeed ; you have never encouraged
him,' said Mrs. Somers emphatically.

' Hadn't we better start now ?' suggested
Bee.

A few steps from the door they were
joined by Mr. West. He was a good-looking
man, fair, with pleasant grey eyes, and a
light brown beard. He had been lately
appointed rector of a parish near Cheynehurst, and soon after he entered upon his
cure he had been attracted by Bee Clare.

He was struck at first by her energy and
industry. He himself was a hardworking

clergyman, to whom his parish was the centre of all his interests ; and when he saw how useful Bee was to her father, it seemed to him that Providence had kindly led him to one who would entirely realize his highest ideal of what a clergyman's wife should be, and he began to pay her attention with a view to annexing her powers of work and her trained capabilities. Her tranquil indifference had stimulated his interest, and he was ending by thinking more of her superficial attractions than her solid merits. He was taking the duty in this little watering-place not in the least to oblige his friend the incumbent.

Mr. West gave Mrs. Somers his arm, and relieved Miss Clare of the old lady's camp-stool and shawl. They walked to the pier, an unpretentious wooden structure, where

Mrs. Somers established herself comfortably to observe all that there was to be seen.

At the seaward end the three boys were fishing with an enthusiastic patience which deserved more encouragement than it received. They were perfectly well now, and no one could be anxious about them.

'I declare,' said Mrs. Somers, 'there is that yacht which I saw out at sea this morning. It has come into the harbour. What a pretty little vessel it is !'

'Very pretty,' said Bee, looking carelessly at the slender, graceful craft. 'I will just go to the end, and see what the boys are doing.'

Mr. West sprang up and prepared to accompany her. She talked pleasantly to him as they went; but Mrs. Somers shook her head despairingly as she looked after them.

'That open friendliness of hers must try the poor fellow awfully.'

The boys were found, each at the end of a line, wearing an expression of absorbed enjoyment, which, as Bee said, showed how modest after all the requirements of the human mind were, and how little could content its desires. They had caught nothing yet, but they were full of hope : they had been assured that fish were to be caught there.

'Yes,' said Bee, 'five years ago a man filled a basket here—isn't that the legend which you put faith in ?'

'It wasn't five years ago; it was this year,' observed Alf, not raising his eyes from the water.

'You'll see that we'll fill a basket too,' said Eustace.

'My dear boy, surely you intend to come home to sleep at least, if not for meals !'

The boys maintained a lofty silence, and Bee, laughing, turned to walk back. She looked very charming as she sauntered slowly along in the warm glow of the afternoon sunlight. She was laughing still, and making a careless remark to Mr. West, when her eye was caught by a figure coming from the other end of the pier. Her sight was long, and the pier was short, but she must be deluded by a chance resemblance. It was only some one tall, and in figure rather like Anthony Fairfax ; it could not be himself in flesh and blood so near her. Yes, it was he !

Bee stopped short in what she was saying ; she forgot that a stranger was by her side, and that appearances must be kept up. All her perceptions were engaged by his neighbourhood: she was only conscious of a wild, overwhelming joy, as she fixed her eyes upon him. He was coming to her; she would hear him speak; he would hold her hand.

'I beg your pardon?' said Mr. West, as she was silent.

She looked up at him with an unseeing, dreamy glance. A soft smile parted her lips—a tender light shone in her eyes.

'Let us sit down here,' she said absently, as if she had not heard him.

Mr. West was a little puzzled by her manner ; but he was highly content to have her company alone a little longer, and he took his place beside her on the seat she chose.

' Isn't the colour of the sea lovely ?' said Bee, in the same absent way.

She could not go to meet him ; she must wait for him. Oh, if only the man beside her would go back to Mrs. Somers, and let their first greeting be undisturbed by strange eyes !

Fairfax was walking slowly, looking away over the sea, as if he had no attention to spare for the people whom he met. Surely he would see her ! He could not pass her without a glance: he could not overlook her altogether. She waited confidently for the meeting of their eyes, watching to see the light of recognition and glad surprise flash into his.

He came near—so near, that two steps would have taken her to his side—and passed on without so much as turning his head. She clutched the back of the seat fast, hurting her fingers with the tight pressure. She felt giddy; there was a mist before her eyes; and she was very cold. She had wondered sometimes if they might meet by chance, and she had imagined how, in such a case, she must behave, and rule her looks and words as if they were 'friends the merest;' but she had never imagined him passing her as a stranger. Had he done it on purpose? Did he think he was debarred from the coldest and most ordinary interchange of civilities with her?

'I—I think I should like to go back,' she said, interrupting some very sensible remarks which Mr. West was making about almsgiving.

'Aren't you well, Miss Clare?' he asked,

in some surprise. ' You look tired ; perhaps the sun has been too much for you.'

If he had only known it, this speech of his roused a warmer feeling in Bee's heart than she had yet experienced for him. She was ardently grateful to him for thinking that she looked only tired, when to her shamed consciousness it seemed that every- one must notice the change in her face, and see how wretched she was, and how hard it was to keep her lips from quivering.

' Yes ; it is very hot. I will go home,' she said hurriedly.

She could not bear to see Fairfax again ; she must escape.

' You had better walk under my um- brella,' said Mr. West ; ' it gives a better shade than your parasol.'

He was putting up the neat umbrella, when Eustace came running.

'Bee—oh, Bee !' he exclaimed; 'here's Mr. Fairfax! Didn't you see him? He's coming to speak to you. Wait a minute. Archie and Alf are bringing him.'

'Your sister is tired,' began Mr. West.

'Oh, she must speak to Mr. Fairfax! You wouldn't like not to — would you, Bee? How ever did you miss seeing him before? Here he is.'

Fairfax was coming towards her, with Alf holding his hand affectionately, while Archie, on the other side, talked with a little shyness. Bee saw that he was quite at his ease, smiling pleasantly at the boys; then he was before her, lifting his hat, and looking at her in the same unembarrassed way. Her own self-possession returned at once; she put out her hand with a frank greeting.

' I was very much surprised to see you just now,' she said.

' I am only here for a day or so.'

' Mr. Fairfax came in that yacht,' said Eustace.

' He's been to Iceland in it,' said Alf, with interest.

Mr. West had retreated, and Bee sat down. Fairfax stood beside her, leaning against the railing.

' Have you been quite well?' he asked, in a rather constrained manner.

' Quite, thank you.' After a brief pause : ' And you ?' she said, with an effort.

' Oh, I have been very well, thank you.'

That was all that they said to each other. There was no opportunity of exchanging anything but formal common-places. The boys stood by and chattered: Mrs. Somers came up, having heard from Mr. West of the sudden appearance of Fairfax, and gave him a voluble greeting.

'How did you manage to pass without my seeing you?' she said. 'Surely you did not mean to cut me?'

'How could I be guilty of such an intention? I did not see either you or Miss Clare.'

'Well, I am glad that we haven't missed you altogether. I am very pleased to see you again. How have you been? You are looking very well. You will come and have tea with me? The Clares are

lodging in the same house, and we will
have tea together.'

Fairfax thanked her, and excused himself.

He could not have the pleasure that
afternoon.

'Well, come later this evening. I can't
ask you to dinner, for we dine early here;
but can't you pay me a visit after your
dinner? Or come to tea to-morrow.'

'Thank you. I am not sure whether
I shall stay over to-morrow.'

'Oh, well,' said Mrs. Somers, with a
slight coldness in her voice, 'if you are
so short of time, of course you cannot spare
any for us.'

'I wish you would come and have tea
with us,' said Alf, looking wistfully at
his friend. 'If you were going to stay

we could come and look at the yacht,' he added diplomatically.

'Well, there is time enough for that,' said Fairfax. 'May they come and pay me a visit there, Miss Clare?'

'Thank you, it will be a great pleasure for them,' she replied steadily, looking at him with a smile.

The boys had to promise Mrs. Somers that they would sit perfectly still in the boat which would take them out to the yacht, and after a little more talk—*very little*—Fairfax carried his young visitors off. The ladies walked down the pier with them; and meeting Mr. West, who was hovering about the end, Mrs. Somers introduced him to Fairfax. Alf suggested that Mr. West's happiness might be increased by an opportunity of viewing the yacht.

'Are you all going?' said Mr. West, with a downcast face.

'Only the boys,' said Bee.

Mr. West brightened up, and hastily thanked Fairfax for the invitation which at Alf's hint he politely gave him. He would walk back with the ladies.

'Is that the Mr. Fairfax that there are such strange stories about?' he asked, glancing after him as they turned their different ways after a leave-taking as brief and dry as the whole conversation had been.

'That is Mr. Fairfax of Cheynehurst,' said Bee, holding her head high.

'Really? I shouldn't have thought it was the same.'

'Why not?' said Miss Clare, with a touch of sharpness in her tone.

'Well, he doesn't look like that sort of character,' said Mr. West, who had forgotten for the moment that he had been told that the Clares had stood by Mr. Fairfax.

'What sort of character? He has been unfortunate, but he didn't deserve it. If you knew him, you would think too highly of his character to mind any gossip,' said Bee deliberately.

'Yes, indeed. You must not run him down in our hearing, Mr. West,' added Mrs. Somers. 'He is a very fine fellow. He has borne his troubles splendidly. I admire him greatly.'

'Oh indeed—I had no intention,' faltered Mr. West, seeing that he had made a mistake, and in abject alarm at the displeasure in Bee's tone. 'I beg your pardon. I did not know that he was such a friend of yours. I have only common report to go by, Mrs. Somers.'

'Of course. But we know Mr. Fairfax, and we can give you a fairer account of him than you can get from common report.'

'I should certainly think your good opinion a sufficient defence against common report,' said Mr. West, wishing that he could see Bee to intimate that her good opinion was included in the 'your.' But she was walking on the other side of Mrs. Somers, and had fallen back out of range of his eyes. 'He is a fine-looking man,' he added, ready to speak well of a man who could not possibly be his rival.

Mrs. Somers assented, and changed the subject. Later, when she and Bee had

had tea and were sitting quietly alone, she asked:

'Bee, is there any reason for Mr. Fairfax's rather peculiar behaviour this afternoon? Why did he refuse to come and see me?'

Taken unawares, Bee started and changed colour.

'Do you know of any reason? Did your papa find out anything about him which caused him to give up his acquaintance?'

'No, no; it wasn't for that!' cried the girl eagerly.

'You are quite sure?'

'Quite. Papa had no cause to think ill of him. Indeed, dear Mrs. Somers, he didn't refuse your invitation for any such reason.'

Mrs. Somers looked only half satisfied.

'Well, it struck me that perhaps that was the case, and I didn't like to think it of him,' she said. 'I stood up for him to Mr. West—I won't encourage such talk without being very sure that it is deserved, but I didn't quite like Mr. Fairfax's behaviour this afternoon. I don't see why he should avoid me.'

'You must not think he wished to avoid you,' said Bee, after a pause. 'Mrs. Somers, I will tell you how it is. He went away from Cheynehurst because he—cared for me.'

Mrs. Somers uttered an exclamation of mingled surprise and regret.

'He loved me,' said Bee firmly and proudly. 'He would have asked me to be his wife if it hadn't been that he thought it wrong to let me share his troubles. He didn't mean me to know how he felt, but he betrayed it one day.'

' Poor fellow !'

' That is all. He gave me up. He told papa he would never come in my way again if he could help it; he would never write to me nor try to keep himself in my mind. So you see he could not come here; he was bound by his word.'

She spoke in a dry, composed tone, looking steadily out of the window.

' Bee, dear child, I am very sorry,' said Mrs. Somers.

' Thank you. But you needn't be sorry : it is an old story,' said Bee. ' I only told you because I did not wish you to be unjust to him. I am sure he was very sorry to seem uncourteous.'

She took up a book and began reading. Mrs. Somers followed her example, feeling a little displeased at receiving such a very meagre account of such an interesting episode. She would have liked much fuller information. She wondered whether Bee had returned Fairfax's love, and how she felt towards him now. Surely she could not speak with such self-command, and meet him so coolly, if any affection lingered. Yet as Mrs. Somers thought of the indifference with which she had treated any man who seemed to admire her, she feared that the affair had gone deeper than was to be desired.

Presently the boys returned, highly delighted with what they had seen, and full of talk about it. They poured long descriptions of the yacht into their sister's ears, to which she listened with the attention which she always had for them. She did not appear to shrink from the subject, nor to take any very deep interest in it. She laughed at their jokes quite gaily. 'Surely,' thought Mrs. Somers, as she heard her laugh, 'she doesn't care for him now, whatever she may have done.'

When the boys had retired to bed, Bee turned back to her book. Presently, about ten, Mrs. Somers asked for the third volume of the novel she was engaged with.

'I don't want it this minute,' she said; 'but I should like to take it up to my room with me.'

She was a very wakeful person, and generally spent the first hours of the night in reading.

'It is in my room. I left it there when I brought the book from the library this morning,' said Bee, rising. 'I will get it.'

She ran lightly upstairs. Once safe in her own room, she shut the door gently behind her, and sank on her knees beside the bed. For five minutes she might relax her guard and let herself look as she would; she might give partial way to the feelings which had risen stormily in her heart. She might think of the meeting that afternoon; she might recall every word and look of his, and feel again the bewilderment and fear which she had felt with him. It had not been safe to do so before; but now she was unwatched.

1

Had he forgotten her? she asked herself.
While she had cherished the thought of
him in her inmost heart, had the thought
of her faded from him? Was it all over?
Was she his love no longer?

It must be so. How else could he have
met her as he did, with no reminder of
the past in look, or tone, or touch? When
he took her hand, there had been no
pressure to thrill her with assurance that
her hand was dearer to him than any
other. There had not been the slightest
trace of emotion or embarrassment in his
manner. He had spoken to her as if she
were an indifferent acquaintance; she who
felt still his last kiss on her lips, and was
the more bound to him because all outward ties were wanting; she who, because
he had been obliged to renounce her, had

OL. III. 55

vowed him in her own heart lifelong
faithfulness. ' Oh Anthony, my Anthony !
aren't you mine still ?' she cried. ' Don't
you want my love now ?'

Perhaps he had forgotten her for the
sake of some one who had charmed him
into forgetfulness of all his gloomy past ;
some woman who knew nothing of it, and
would never remind him of it. He might
have been glad to put the thought of
Beatrice away, as part of the unhappiness
which he tried to escape. It would be
only natural if he had. She was so connected with his humiliation, that his love
for her must be painful. Yes ; his
thoughts of her must have given him
bitter mortification, and stung him with
remembrance many a time.

And he was not bound to her in any

way—not by honour, or promise, or hope. His honour lay in renouncing her; his promise had been not to see her again. He was sure to turn to another woman; he could not waste his life in devotion to one who was hopelessly lost to him. She ought to be glad if he had found some one who could make him happy. 'But I am not glad,' she told herself fiercely. She was selfish, perhaps; but she could not bear the thought of giving up her shadowy rights of possession in him. It tortured her with jealousy to think of another woman making him forget her. She could not try to overcome the passionate misery which racked her, as she fancied some one else at his side.

She had not realized before what their parting meant. She had not felt that they

were set apart till this day. She had clung
to the hope that some day everything would
come right, and they would be restored to
each other. She had not allowed herself
to repine at their separation. It was only
for a time ; and that confidence had helped
her pride to keep her cheerful. She would
not appear sad, for Anthony would be
blamed for her sadness, and her father
should not think that it did her harm
to love him. She had never given him
up. She would love him as she was sure
he would love her, till somehow the bar-
riers between them were removed.

But now that hope broke in her grasp.
It might be fulfilled too late to bring
Anthony back to her.

She rose presently with a start of fear
lest she had stayed too long, and went

to the window where the table was on which she had left the book. The window was open, and the blind was not drawn; and she lingered in the current of cool air, trying to compose herself into a fitting serenity to appear before Mrs. Somers. The air was refreshing, and there was a soothing influence in the sight of the sea lying calm in the clear light of the moon.

As she looked out, her eye fell on a man's figure standing on the path which ran at the top of the cliff past the house, and she moved back a little as if he could have seen her behind the muslin curtain.

She recognised him directly. He was watching the house where she was ; he had come as near her as he could. She clasped

her hands tight, and a low sob of exquisite
relief and happiness broke from her.   She
watched the tall figure with eager straining
eyes.   He walked slowly past, then he
turned and came back.   Was ever sound so
sweet to her ears as his footstep crunching
down the pebbles ?

She had been quite wrong.   He did care
for her still ; cared so much that he could
act in this lover-like, romantic fashion.   All
her dark fancies were dispersed.

He had been cold that afternoon because
he thought it his duty.   Had he not bound
himself not to attempt to keep up her interest
in him ?   The meeting which she had been
breaking her heart over made her proud now
that he would do what he thought right, at
any cost to himself.   She would not see him
again, but she was content.

There was a bright rose-colour on her cheeks, and a deep light shining in her eyes, when she went downstairs at last.

'Here is the book, Mrs. Somers.'

'Thank you, my dear. Bee, will you let me ask you a question? I loved your mother very dearly, and I had you in my arms when you were a day old. I don't speak out of curiosity.'

'Dear Mrs. Somers, of course not. Ask me what you like.'

'Is this,' said Mrs. Somers vaguely, 'the reason why you are so certain that Mr. West has no chance?'

Bee's colour deepened a little, but she looked unfalteringly at the questioner.

'Yes,' she said simply. 'I can't care for anybody now but Anthony Fairfax.'

Mrs. Somers sighed.

'You must give up planning good matches for me,' went on Bee. 'I am quite hopeless.'

'But, my dear child, if he gave you up, what is the good of thinking of him any longer ?'

'I can't help myself,' replied Bee, with a break in her voice. 'I couldn't give up thinking of him if I tried.'

'It is very sad for you both,' said Mrs. Somers, thinking that Mr. Clare must have managed matters very badly.

'It is worse for him—a thousand times worse than for me!' cried Bee energetically. 'I have my home, and plenty to do, and I am fairly happy—quite happy enough for working-days ; but he is alone, and he has had all the bitterness of that terrible misfortune.'

'And you will make all your youth unhappy for the sake of a man who will never be in a position to marry you?'

'I am not unhappy. You must not pity me, Mrs. Somers. You must do me the justice to confess that I am not in the least like the heroine of a pathetic love-story. I have no "hopes of dying broken-hearted."'

'I should trust not,' interjected Mrs. Somers, not knowing the quotation.

'And there is no interesting sadness about me.'

She looked so full of life and youth and hope as the lamplight fell on her smiling face, that Mrs. Somers forgot her sage objections and fears, or at least felt that it was useless to urge them.

CHAPTER II.

'But in somewise all things wear round betimes
And wind up well.'

SWINBURNE.

NEXT morning Mrs. Somers proposed privately to Bee that they should make an excursion to a place a few miles off, which they intended to visit. But Bee did not appear willing to go.

'I know why you think of it to-day,' she said, with a smile which provoked and perplexed Mrs. Somers ; 'but it is quite unnecessary to take precautions. I shall not see him. He will take very good care of that.'

'You seem pleased to think so. You look quite radiant on the expectation.'

Bee laughed.

'He promised, you know, and he will keep his word. I am not going to make myself miserable about it. I told you last night that I was not unhappy,' she rejoined.

'You are the very strangest girl,' said Mrs. Somers.

But Bee had her way, and the day was spent in the little town. It would be only one day, fortunately, that she would have the neighbourhood of her lover to disturb her equanimity. The morning passed in the usual way. Bee and the boys went for a long stroll on the sands first, and then she joined Mrs. Somers on the promenade, and they walked about a little, and sat down a great deal. But whatever they did, Bee's eyes were always straying off to the yacht. They rested on it with a peculiar expression—not sad, as one would have expected, but a satisfied, peaceful look.

Mr. West joined them, and was much discouraged by the way in which he was received. Mrs. Somers did not appear so glad to see him as usual, and Miss Clare was taciturn and dreamy to an unprecedented extent. She was very lovely that morning; that absent, pensive look made her face very sweet. Mr. West wondered jealously once or twice whether that expression was a tribute to some admirer. But no ; he had lived nine months in the next parish to Cheynehurst, and he had never heard of any

love affair. He had no rival that he need fear.
He had been a little alarmed at first sight
of Mr. Fairfax ; but of course any entangle-
ment there was out of the question. It was
only a mood, and a very charming mood
too, thought Mr. West, who was in the state
of mind which declares, ' What you do still
betters what is done.'

' Were the boys able to tear themselves
away from the yacht in good time?' he
asked.

' Oh yes,' replied Bee ; ' they came back
about nine.'

' They have talked of nothing else in my
hearing since,' said Mrs. Somers.

' They are full of technical terms, which
are Greek to me,' said Bee. ' It makes
their talk rather difficult to follow, especially as now and then they disagree about

the meaning of a word, and stop to argue
it out.'

' I was wondering whether it would do to
ask Mr. Fairfax for a donation to the
church,' said Mr. West.   He was restoring
his church, and he found it very hard work
to raise the necessary money.   ' He owns a
little land in my parish, I believe, and I
shall never have such an opportunity of
asking him again.'

' Oh, ask him by all means,' said Bee.
' He will give you a good donation.'

' He is very well off, I believe.'

' And very liberal, too,' said Bee, as
calmly as she might have spoken about Mr.
West himself.

' Had I better send a note, or go out to
the yacht ?' mused the clergyman.

He attended them back to the house,

and on the way he talked of the church
and his many anxieties connected with it.
He had some plans which he wished to
show Miss Clare, and at the door, when he
took leave, he proposed to bring them in
the evening for her inspection.

'Thank you,' said Bee; 'but I don't
think to-night will be a good time. If you
would bring them another day——'

'Certainly. To-morrow, then ; and I
can tell you whether Mr. Fairfax has justified your confidence in him.'

Bee's smile was faint as she said good-
morning, and she hurried upstairs to
struggle against a strong inclination to
cry.

It was strange that Mr. West's talk of
him made her feel how far off he was with
a poignancy which nearly broke down her

self-control. That a mere stranger could tell her of his doings, and she must only hear of him in this fashion !

That afternoon she refused to go out. She pleaded fatigue as a reason for staying indoors; and Mrs. Somers, seeing her pallor and listlessness, left her in peace. Of course, this was the reaction after the agitation of seeing him unexpectedly. The poor child must feel depressed ; it was a much more natural frame of mind than her excitement last night.

All the exalted confidence which Bee had felt then had forsaken her suddenly. She was lonely and dejected; too miserable to be comforted by anything so unsubstantial as her lover's faithfulness at a distance. She yearned for his presence; she would have given all her thoughts of him for five minutes' speech. The silence chilled and oppressed her; it must drive them further and further away from each other.

She sat watching the yacht with an aching longing for him. Why must they keep apart? If he really loved her, how could he bear the separation without doing his utmost to win her? The reasons for this loneliness seemed weak before her strong longing. Oh! it was piteous that this was all she could have, that the mere sight of the vessel which held him gave her pleasure, and she dreaded to lose even that!

There came a knock at the door, and the maid put her head in and said:

' A gentleman wants to see you, miss.'

Bee sat up in the easy-chair in which she had thrown herself back, and after a moment's pause said languidly:

' Show him in.'

It must be Mr. West, come on some pre-
text or other. She was strongly inclined
to send him away ; but it would scarcely
do, and it mattered little whether he bored
her or not while she was in this dispirited
state. He could not add to her dull
wretchedness. And the infliction would be
brief, as he could not stay in Mrs. Somers'
absence.

She raised her eyes with a cold indifference as her visitor entered, and started to
her feet with a low cry of amazement. It
was Anthony Fairfax who was coming
towards her. She half stretched out her
hands to him ; then she drew back a step,
and her hands fell at her side as she remembered with a rush how he had greeted her
yesterday.

'Mrs. Somers is out,' she said hastily.

'I came to see you, not Mrs. Somers,' he answered, stopping at a few paces from her. 'I came to tell you some news. I am cleared.'

'You are—what?' she said hoarsely.

'I am cleared; I can prove that I was innocent.'

She looked at him in a bewildered way.

'But—I can't understand. You said— yesterday——'

'I only heard an hour ago. I could come to you then.'

'You are cleared?' she cried. 'Oh, thank God!'

She sank down in her chair, and burst into passionate sobs. The change was overwhelming. He made no attempt to approach; he stood silent, watching her.

'I can't help it,' she said at last, drying her eyes and smiling through her tears. 'It isn't the way to wish you joy, but you took me by surprise,' she faltered, wondering why he looked so strangely at her.

'Is it too late?' he said, as if he had difficulty in speaking.

She looked up at him inquiringly.

'Are you free?'

'Oh yes!' in a tone of amazement, which was a sufficient answer to any fears he might have entertained on that score.

'And you have not changed?' he asked, taking her hands. 'My own, my own, at last!' as he read her answer in her face.

'You are quite cleared?' she said, when her tumult of joy and surprise had subsided a little ; and it seemed less wonderful to have him there.

'Entirely. Your father will be satisfied. He will consent now, surely.'

'Of course. It was only for that that he objected. And you thought more of it than he did. I shall always believe that if you had made a good fight for me you would have succeeded in the long-run,' she said, smiling half tenderly, half mockingly. 'But you preferred to give me up in true heroic fashion.'

'Very heroic. There never was anything done more unwillingly and grudgingly than my leaving you. When I was in the deepest depths of wretchedness about you, I used to doubt whether after all it had not been wrong. I felt now and then that I had acted tamely in not making a good fight for you.'

'Did you want me?'

' Want you ?' The arms round her tightened their hold. ' I was mad with longing for you sometimes—just for a sight of you. It was more than I could bear to remember that I had lost you.'

' Ah, don't think of it !' she said quickly, half frightened by the glimpse of suffering which his words gave her. ' It is all over now. You haven't told me how the truth came out,' she added, to lead his thoughts away.

' I am afraid that I am not equal to giving you a full account. I was too much excited to get an exact idea of the way in which the discovery was made ; and when I knew I was cleared, the only thing I could think of was that I must hurry to you with the news. I could not wait five minutes longer than I could help to know whether it would give you back to me.'

' You didn't really think that I might have changed ?'

' I was miserably afraid that you might have forgotten me. When I saw you yesterday talking to that man——'

' Oh, Anthony !' reproachfully.

' I thought what a good thing it would be for you to like a person of irreproachable respectability ; and how your friends would encourage it, and approve; and how I had given you up, and told you that I could be glad if you forgot me ; and—well, my thoughts were not enjoyable.'

' I thought of you in pretty much the same way. You were so cool yesterday, that I fancied you were forgetting.'

' What else could I be when I was

hating that man so intensely because he could be with you, and I was banished? It was difficult to speak to you at all. And you did not reassure me. You were as indifferent, it seemed to me, as when I saw you first at Cheynehurst.'

' You little knew how I envied the boys, because they could see more of you than I could. But how did you hear the news?'

'Joe Dixon brought it. He made the discovery in some way, but I did not hear the story out. He shall tell you all about it himself—that will be a reward he will value.'

' Where is he?'

'I left him on the yacht. Now I think of it, I behaved very cavalierly to him,' said Fairfax. 'I only thought of seeing

you, and getting put out of my pain. I
barely thanked the poor fellow—I was so
afraid that the news had come too late.
But he will forgive me for my abruptness
when he knows that it was on your account. I must go back, and hear him at
length.'

'Couldn't he come here? I should like
to hear his first full story.'

'Yes; that will be the best plan. I
will send and ask him to come this evening.'

He went away to despatch the message,
absurdly reluctant to leave her even for a
brief half-hour; and Bee was left alone to
rejoice in the sunshine which had burst
out on her so suddenly, and to shed some
more tears in her ecstasy of relief and
happiness.

She was lost in a blissful reverie when Mrs. Somers came in.

'I hope you have been resting, my love?'

'Yes, a little,' said Bee mechanically.

Mrs. Somers saw the tears on her cheeks, and carefully looked away from her.

'You will feel better for some tea,' she said cheerfully.

'Never mind the tea just now,' said Bee, arresting the hand she was laying on the bell-rope. 'Wait, please. I have something to tell you. Don't look so gravely at me. I am crying for joy. I am so glad, dear Mrs. Somers—so glad!'

CHAPTER III.

'What o' the way to the end ?—the end crowns all.'
The Ring and the Book.

JOE DIXON was a proud man that day, and his elation reached its height when he was sent for to tell his story to Miss Clare. To shine as the hero of the affair before her, and to witness her interest and delight, gave his pleasure in his embassy the last exquisite touch of perfection.

He presented himself at the house

punctually, and he told his tale to the audience of three, launching out into greater length under the influence of the ladies' presence. He modestly prefaced his narrative with the declaration that it wasn't anything of a story ; but he could not deny himself the satisfaction of making the most of what he had to relate, and he answered with much detail every question which was put to him. His account may be condensed with advantage.

When he left Cheynehurst, he went back to Middleton, moved to that step by two motives. His betrayal of Fairfax's secret had thrown him into a fit of remorse, in which he repented indiscriminately of many things unconnected with his offence ; and he felt that it would be an act of penance towards his wife to return to the town

which she had never wished to leave. He
also wished to live there, because he
thought that he might pick up some clue
which should bring the guilt home to the
offender, for whom Fairfax had been made
the scapegoat. He was resolved to devote
himself to clear Fairfax, if it was possible.
Nothing else would make up for the mischief he had done. It would be a fine
thing if he could set Mr. Fairfax straight
with the world, and beat the detectives on
their own ground ; and he set to work
with a good deal of confidence ; his
arrogant belief in himself being strengthened
—almost ennobled—by his eager desire to
succeed.

Fairfax, at his request, had given him a
brief outline of his story; and Joe set
himself to work to watch the cousin, and

learn all he could about him. Each fact
he learnt seemed to put the possibility
of success in his enterprise a little further
off. Mr. Walter Lingen was a blameless
person, of whom everyone spoke well.
His only excesses were in medicine; his
only extraordinary expenses in the way
of doctors' fees; for he was very delicate
in health. In his invalid existence there
was no room for extravagance and dissipa-
tion; no encouragement to hope that he
would go so deep in bad courses that his
career would be at length laid open to the
world. It seemed preposterous to think
of bringing any disreputable secrets of his
to light.

Joe at last gave up his quest in despair,
seeing, as he grimly observed, that he ' was
a vast more likely to die quoting texts

than to make a confession that he'd been a thief.'

He had given it up for months, when a chance ('Eternal God that chance did guide') made him take it up again. He was engaged in painting old Mr. Lingen's house, and one afternoon he stayed for a few minutes after five to finish a bit of ceiling.

In the quiet he heard a few words spoken in the next room, which he knew was Walter Lingen's sitting - room. It opened into the room where Joe was engaged, and the door between had been pulled to by some one passing through, but not latched. Joe heard plainly something said in a rough voice about 'that business of your cousin's,' which would have been meaningless to anyone else, but which was full of significance to him. He stopped and listened, and heard a few more cautious sentences which made him sure that Fairfax was referred to.

When the subject was changed, he withdrew noiselessly, and loitered about the house till he saw Walter Lingen's visitor come out; then he followed him to the next house he entered. Fortunately for Joe's purpose, this was a public-house. Joe went in too, and found out the man's name. It was Cox—the name of the receiver of the notes, who had been the principal witness against Fairfax, who had disappeared from the town after the trial, and was not to be found anywhere when Fairfax set inquiries on foot. Joe fully appreciated the importance of this discovery; and at once made acquaintance with

Mr. Cox, and cultivated him spite of the lofty swagger by which that gentleman marked his recognition of the wide difference which separated him from a working-man.

What Mr. Cox's calling had been when he did labour to get his own living, nobody knew. It was formerly understood in Middleton that he had some connection with racing. He now appeared to have given that up; but he had not provided himself with any visible means of subsistence. He was hanging about, doing nothing, and his social prejudices were not proof against the generosity with which Joe treated him to spirits and tobacco.

He soon unbent to such a useful friend, and Joe watched him patiently, trying to find out the best way of extorting or worming a confession of the truth from him. It was rather a desperate undertaking, for the man must accuse himself of perjury if he said what Joe longed to hear.

At first Mr. Cox, while very willing to drink at Joe's expense, was caution itself in his talk. Joe persisted in his attentions. He was encouraged by observing that Mr. Cox was extremely shabby and short of money, and occasionally grumbled savagely about the mean way in which he was treated by some people from whom he had deserved better things. Walter Lingen evidently had failed in the liberality which Mr. Cox had expected. This was well. The less he had to lose by open confession the better.

One evening Mr. Cox paid a visit to Joe at his own house, and in the course of the talk as they sat alone, he grumbled more freely and openly than usual at his hard lot and the straits to which a too generous trust in the promises of others had reduced him. He had been ruined by this over-ready confidence, and he repented with all his heart of the weakness of nature which had made him impecu·nious.

Joe artfully sympathized and led him on; but even when he was most fluent in his complaints of ingratitude and faithlessness, Mr. Cox ingeniously avoided saying a word that could give Joe the opening he looked for. He kept far enough away from particulars, and rambled on in vague discourse, which could not excite in any-

one without Joe's knowledge a suspicion
that the services he was inadequately paid
for were not of a moral and beneficent
nature.

Joe listened in growing impatience, and
presently said quietly:

'Ay, it's too bad of young Lingen to
let you want, after all that's come and
gone between you. He ought to do
more in return for what you did for
him.'

He had carefully calculated this speech,
and he was rewarded by seeing its
immediate effect. The man looked
thunder - struck, and stared with drop-
ping jaw and wide eyes.

'What do you know about young
Lingen?' was all he could say.

'Oh, I know plenty,' said Joe deliberately. 'I heard you and him talking about his cousin the other day when I was painting in their house.'

Mr. Cox no doubt could remember talks which were much more unreserved than the one Joe had overheard. He turned a little paler.

· I don't believe a word of it,' he said, rising.

' Would you like to know what I heard ? I'll repeat it if you like ?' said Joe, preparing to draw freely on his inventive powers.

' Hold your tongue !' cried the other, glancing nervously at the door. ' I'm going. I've had enough of this.'

He strode out. Joe remained in his place, feeling the excitement of one who has made a bold move, and is watching for its result. If this stroke failed, how was he to proceed ?

Cox banged the door after him, walked away a few paces, thrust his hands into his pockets; and as if their condition 'gave him pause,' stopped, pondered for a minute, then turned round and came back. Joe kept silence as he entered and sat down, pulling his chair near to his host's.

'Look here,' he said, in a cautious undertone. 'What's your game? You've found this out—what do you want to be up to ?'

'I want to have the rights of the business known, and the innocent cleared,' replied Joe. 'I mean to see young Lingen tried for theft and disgraced before everybody, as his cousin was.'

'That's it, is it? I say, I'll turn Queen's evidence. Nobody can touch me then. I'll split on that——' here a very uncomplimentary if forcible description of Mr. Walter Lingen. 'He shan't get me into prison, if I know it. I've done enough for him. Just bring me forward as a witness.'

Finding Mr. Cox so well-disposed, Joe had no difficulty in extracting from him an account of Walter Lingen's misdoings which was very satisfactory. The man was eager to tell all he could and save himself; and he had, besides, a vindictive pleasure in turning on his patron.

A statement of the truth about Anthony Lingen's affair was written out and signed before witnesses that same evening; and next day Joe laid it before old Mr. Lingen, who of course refused at first to believe a word of it. But he soon passed from scornful denial to sullen acknowledgment of the part his son had played. He was in a piteous position; and the struggle between his sense of justice and his fatherly affection would have ended in the complete defeat of his conscience, if Joe had not been at hand to insist that Anthony must be cleared. Mr. Cox was willing to take a handsome sum of money and leave the country; but Joe was not to be silenced. He was a man whom it was out of the question to bribe; he was not to be softened by the most pathetic representations that any stirring-up of the affair in Walter Lingen's state of health would probably hasten his end; he was proof even against a proposal that if Walter was only allowed to die in peace (he could not possibly live long), full justice should be done afterwards. Mr. Fairfax should not suffer an hour that could be prevented.

At last, in a grudging, half-hearted way, the old man agreed to clear his kinsman. There could be no question of prosecuting the real offender; but he would make known that he had discovered Anthony's innocence, and a statement to that effect was published in the newspapers of the town.

Joe, triumphant in his success, hurried to inform Fairfax as soon as a letter from Bob told him where he was to be found. He claimed the office of bearing the good news as his right, and he brought with him a letter from old Mr. Lingen, which he had demanded as his credentials.

Fairfax handed it over to Bee, when
Joe had ended his story. She read the
brief, formal communication with some
anger.

' Why, he scarcely says he is sorry !' she
exclaimed at the end.

' I don't believe he is, ma'am,' said Joe.
' He's mad that his son should be such
a blackguard—I beg your pardon, Miss
Clare,' said Joe, pulling up in dismay.
' I didn't mean to use such a word before
you.'

' Oh, Miss Clare can forgive a little
strong language on the subject !' said
Mrs. Somers.

' He's awfully cut up about his son, and
he's angry that he's the culprit instead
of Mr. Fairfax. He is sorry that Mr.
Fairfax didn't deserve it—that's how he

feels,' continued Joe. 'He's believed in that son, and now he finds he has been taken in completely.'

'Well, he must feel having to disgrace his own son,' said Mrs. Somers, with an attempt to do justice to a father in such a position.

'Oh, the son's safe enough!' said Joe, in a tone of strong disgust. 'He's too ill to be punished. That's just how such folks get out of everything. You can't touch a man that can get up a fit of coughing if you give him a piece of your mind.'

'Is he so ill?' asked Bee.

Joe made an eloquent grimace.

'He's ill enough to find it come in uncommon useful. I suppose he has something the matter with him,' he added

candidly. ' He is white and thin, and he
has to keep quiet and go abroad every
winter. But he can make the most of
it.'

' You certainly can't do anything to a
man in that state,' said Mrs. Somers almost
regretfully.

' You would not wish it,' said Bee, looking up at her lover with a proud confidence
shining in her eyes.

His face had grown stern and clouded as
he listened to Joe's narrative. The old
hateful wrong lived again, and cast its
shadow over him; he suffered in memory
the desolation it had brought upon him.
Now, as Bee's glance sought his, he smiled,
and all the gloom disappeared.

' No ; he must be left alone,' he said
almost carelessly.

He did not care to think about his cousin one way or another just then.

Any desire for revenge must have been quenched by the approach of death. But Fairfax had no such desire at that moment. His injury belonged to the past; it was over and done with. Let it go with the shadows of that time; let the dark, chill, unsubstantial presence fade away before his new dawn.

This was real and true and lasting; the love that looked out of Bee's eyes, the faith that had held by him through all, the sweetness that would bless every day of his life to come. Who would waste a thought willingly on the things that lay behind when so much was before?

Later that evening he was alone with Bee. The lamp was not lit, and from the window they watched the moon rise in the clear sky. His arm was round Bee, and she had laid her head on his shoulder.

'Anthony,' she said, 'you must be very happy now.'

'I shall be,' he replied.

'You ought to be happier than most people; there is so much to make up to you,' she continued softly. 'You have lost seven years, and you must have them back again. Promise me that you will try to forget everything that has made you sad, and you will let me make you quite bright.'

'Like yourself? My darling, I fear you will have a hard task. The seven years have set their mark on me and made me moody. I will do my best to forget; but after all, I am not a very suitable husband for you. I am not sure that it is not selfish to ask you to come to me.'

'It is too late to think of that now. You know you couldn't give me up. You can't do without me.'

'No, I cannot,' he said, drawing her closer and kissing her passionately. 'How could a man who has been in purgatory give up heaven? But it might be better for you,' he added.

It was only a half-earnest suggestion of doubt, not deep or real enough to trouble his joy.

'I wish you would not talk such wild nonsense,' said Bee, in a rather aggrieved tone. 'I am so glad that everything has come right, and you ought to be too glad to talk of leaving me even as a flight of fancy.'

' Am I not glad ? I am not quite sure that it is all real yet. Only yesterday I was nothing to you—I had not even a right to think of you ; and now I may worship you, and you are all my own. You need not be anxious about my happiness, dearest. I have my heart's desire at last.'

'If it depends on me, you shall be happy,' she said earnestly. 'But I want you to be more than solemnly happy; you must be bright, too.'

' You shall make me just what you please,' he answered, smiling.

THE END.

BILLING AND SONS, PRINTERS, GUILDFORD.
G., C. & Co.